The Orphan Prodigy of Pembroke Manor

Sophia Watts

Copyright © 2024 by **Sophia Watts**

All rights reserved. No part of this publication may be reproduced, distributed or transmitted in any form or by any means, without prior written permission.

Contents

Chapter One 1

Chapter Two..15

Chapter Three...31

Chapter Four 55

Chapter Five...71

Chapter Six...87

Chapter Seven 107

Chapter Eight 117

Chapter Nine 133

Chapter Ten..149

Chapter Eleven...159

Chapter Twelve..175

Chapter Thirteen 189

Chapter Fourteen...199

Chapter Fifteen..209

Chapter One

The grey dawn light filtered through the tall, narrow windows of Hawthornfield Orphanage, casting long shadows across the bare floorboards of the dormitory. Charlotte Brindley stifled a yawn as the shrill chime of the old grandfather clock signaled the start of another day. Around her, the other girls stirred reluctantly from their thin pallets, the chill of the morning air biting through their threadbare nightgowns.

With practiced efficiency, the children dressed and made their beds, their every movement governed by the regimented schedule that ruled their lives. No laughter or idle chatter filled the room - only the occasional creak of a bedframe and the muted shuffle of slippered feet. Charlotte smoothed the worn fabric of her sheets, her brow furrowed in concentration. Though she was but twelve years old, the rhythms of this place had become as familiar to her as her own heartbeat.

A sharp rap at the dormitory door startled the children to attention. "Girls! You have but five minutes to make yourselves presentable for breakfast. Any dawdling will be met with consequences," barked the stern voice of Mrs. Higgins, the matron. The older woman's lips were set in a thin, disapproving line as she swept her critical gaze over the room, her eyes lingering on Charlotte's neat, tidy bed.

Hastening to finish, the children filed out of the dormitory and down the echoing corridors, their footsteps muffled by the threadbare runner that stretched the length of the hall. The smell of porridge and stale bread wafted from the kitchen, mingling with the sour tang of disinfectant that clung to the air. At the end of the hallway, the dining hall loomed, its high ceilings and rows of scarred wooden benches lending an aura of institutional austerity.

As the children took their seats, their conversation was limited to the barest of necessities. Heads bent over their bowls, they ate in sullen silence, their spoons clinking against the crockery. Charlotte poked at her porridge, her appetite diminished by the joyless atmosphere. Though she had called this place home for as long as she could remember, she had never grown accustomed to the relentless monotony and lack of affection that permeated every aspect of life at Hawthornfield.

Charlotte's eyes drifted to the high windows, where the morning light was just beginning to strengthen. Once breakfast was finished, the children would be dismissed to their chores and lessons - the same monotonous routine that governed every waking hour.

After the meal, Mrs. Higgins barked orders, dispatching the girls to their various tasks. Charlotte found herself assigned to the laundry, trudging down the corridor with a heavy basket of soiled linens. The soapy steam and rhythmic slosh of scrubbing boards filled the humid air, the chatter of the other girls a muffled drone in the background. Charlotte worked methodically, her hands growing red and chapped from the constant immersion in hot water.

When the laundry was tended to, she made her way to the schoolroom, the journal and stubby pencil she had secreted away earlier that morning tucked into the pocket of her plain pinafore. The tutor, an elderly clergyman with a wheezing cough, droned on about foreign history and the importance of obedience, his lecture punctuated by the scratch of charcoal on slates. Charlotte dutifully copied down the facts, her mind drifting to the small, hidden compartment in her bedside table where she stashed some of her treasured mechanical parts.

During the brief recreation period after lessons, Charlotte would often steal away to the empty storeroom, losing herself in the intricate workings of a broken pocket watch or a wind-up toy. The repetitive motions of cleaning and repairing the discarded trinkets soothed her, and she took pride in coaxing them back to life. It was the only time she felt truly alive, her fingers deftly manipulating the tiny gears and springs with a deftness that belied her young age.

But all too soon, the chime of the clock signaled the end of playtime, and Charlotte would reluctantly return the toys to their hiding place, her heart heavy. The rest of the afternoon was spent on more chores - scrubbing floors, polishing shoes, mending torn uniforms. By the time the dinner bell rang, she was exhausted, her muscles aching from the ceaseless labour. She'd have to wait until tomorrow to return.

Charlotte's fingers worked deftly as she cracked open the casing of the ornate brass clock, her brow furrowed in concentration. The rhythmic ticking had caught her ear earlier that day, the sound stuttering and irregular. Now, with the delicate mechanism exposed, she could see the issue - a single gear had slipped slightly out of alignment, throwing the whole assembly off.

Carefully, she used the tiny tools she had secreted away to nudge the offending gear back into place, her breath held as she tested the movement. A satisfied smile curved her lips as the clock resumed its steady pulse, the hands sweeping around the face with renewed purpose.

It was in these private moments, tucked away in the shadowy storeroom, that Charlotte felt a true sense of freedom. Here, she could lose herself in the intricate workings of discarded toys and trinkets, her nimble fingers coaxing them back to life. The monotony of the orphanage's rigid schedule faded away, replaced by the soothing hum of machinery and the quiet triumph of a repair well executed.

With a wistful sigh, she returned the clock to its place on the dusty shelf, smoothing a finger over the ornate casing. If only she could find a way to put her talents to greater use, to break free of the stifling confines of Hawthornfield and the unforgiving gaze of Mrs. Higgins. But for now, these stolen moments of tinkering would have to suffice, a secret rebellion against the sterile, joyless existence that had been imposed upon her.

As the chime of the dinner bell once again echoed through the halls, Charlotte straightened her pinafore and schooled her features into an expression of dutiful compliance. With one last wistful glance at the rows of discarded treasures, she turned and hurried to join the other girls, her mind already contemplating the next broken toy that might come her way.

The dining hall was a sea of starched aprons and polished shoes, the air thick with the aroma of boiled vegetables and stale bread. Charlotte slid into her usual seat, casting a furtive glance towards the head of the table where Mrs. Higgins presided like an iron-willed queen.

As the meal progressed in stony silence, Charlotte found her attention drifting back to the trinkets she had left behind in the dim storeroom. The satisfying click as the clock's gears had realigned, the way the hands had swept around the face with renewed purpose - these were the moments that made the endless tedium of the orphanage bearable. Other girls found other ways to distract themselves. Most of them did. And Charlotte had hers.

Unbidden, her hand strayed to the pocket of her pinafore, fingers tracing the familiar outline of a delicate music box she had discovered the previous week. The mechanism was rusted and the tune now only a faint, tinkling echo, but Charlotte cherished the object, imagining the melody as it must have once sounded.

"Charlotte Brindley."

The stern voice cut through her reverie, and Charlotte's head snapped up to meet Mrs. Higgins' piercing gaze. "Yes, ma'am?" she replied, cursing the tremor in her voice.

"I could not help but notice you fidgeting in your seat." Mrs. Higgins' lips thinned into a disapproving line. "One would think a girl of your age would have learned the importance of stillness and composure by now."

Charlotte swallowed hard, her heart pounding in her ears. "I-I'm sorry, ma'am. It won't happen again."

"See that it doesn't." Mrs. Higgins' gaze swept over the other girls, her expression brooking no argument. "As I've told you all before, obedience and practical skills are the foundations upon which a respectable young woman is built. Fanciful interests in such...trinkets," she said, her eyes narrowing, "are a waste of time and energy better spent on your duties."

Before Charlotte could react, Mrs. Higgins reached across the table and plucked the music box from her pocket, holding it aloft with a sneer. "This sort of frivolous nonsense has no place here. Back to the storeroom with it, where it belongs."

Charlotte's stomach lurched as she watched the precious object disappear into Mrs. Higgins' grasp, a lump rising in her throat. "But, ma'am, I-
_"

"Enough." Mrs. Higgins' voice was sharp, cutting off any further protest. "You would do well to remember your place, child. The sooner you learn to put aside such childish whims, the better prepared you'll be for the realities of the world beyond these walls."

Charlotte waited until the dormitory had fallen silent, the soft snores of the other girls the only sound interrupting the stillness. Careful not to disturb them, she slipped from her bed, her stockinged feet barely making a sound as she padded across the worn floorboards.

Retrieving a candle from the bedside table, she lit it, the flickering flame casting a warm glow that guided her steps. She moved with a sense of purpose, making her way to the far corner of the room, leading to one of the few room extensions in any of the dorms, where a worn wooden chest sat silently and forgotten around the corner, its surface covered in a thin layer of dust. Yet another place to hide her secrets.

Kneeling before it, Charlotte lifted the lid, revealing a trove of discarded mechanical parts, tarnished tools, and the precious music box Mrs. Higgins had confiscated. Being who she was, she had snuck it back here quickly. Reverently, she ran her fingers over the delicate casing, feeling the rough edges and imagining once more the song it had once played.

This was her secret space, a hidden sanctuary where she could truly be herself. Here, she was not just another orphan, destined to be molded into a proper young lady. Here, she was free to tinker, to explore, to let her imagination soar.

Well, here and the storeroom. Her private getaways.

Carefully, she extracted the music box and set it aside, her gaze sweeping over the other treasures. A tarnished pocket watch, its hands frozen in time. A broken clockwork doll, its porcelain face cracked but its intricate mechanisms still intact. Each item held the promise of potential, of a future where her skills could be put to use in ways that went beyond the confines of the orphanage. A gift to herself in fixing, a gift to others in owning.

If anyone ever would. But she would do her part, at least.

Charlotte's slender fingers danced across the familiar pieces, her mind already whirring with ideas. She selected a screwdriver and set to work on the music box, determined to coax the long-silenced melody back to life. The rhythmic click of the screws and the gentle hum of the gears were a soothing symphony, a reminder that even in this bleak place, she could find solace in the act of creation.

As she worked, a feeling of calm washed over her. Here, in this secret space, she was the master of her own destiny, free to explore the boundless possibilities that lay beyond the orphanage walls.

Her mind was free.

And with each turn of the screwdriver, each adjustment to the delicate mechanisms, Charlotte's resolve hardened. Someday, she would leave this place behind and make her mark on the world, her skills and determination as her steadfast companions.

The next day, Charlotte sat by the small, crooked window, peering out at the world beyond the Orphanage's austere walls. Sunlight spilled through the grimy panes, casting a warm glow that was so foreign to the cold, institutional corridors she navigated daily.

Outside, the streets bustled with life – people hurried along, their coats billowing behind them, their voices mingling in a symphony of laughter and chatter. Carriages rumbled past, their horses' hooves rhythmically striking the cobblestones. The air itself seemed to thrum with a sense of possibility, a stark contrast to the stagnant monotony that permeated the Orphanage.

What must it be like?

Charlotte's fingers traced the weathered wooden frame, her eyes drinking in the sights with a hunger that could not be sated. How she longed to be out there, to feel the wind on her face and the freedom of the open sky above her. The Orphanage, with its high walls and strict regimen, felt more like a prison than a home, and Charlotte's heart ached to explore the world beyond.

Unconsciously, her gaze drifted to a passing carriage, its elegant design and polished exterior a world away from the utilitarian functionality of the Orphanage. She imagined the wealthy passengers within, their lives filled with possibility and privilege, unbound by the constraints that shackled her to this bleak existence.

A faint sigh escaped her lips, and she pressed her forehead against the cool glass, wishing she could will herself through the window and into that bustling world beyond. If only she could escape the narrow confines of her life, to discover the wonders that surely awaited her. The ticking of the clock on the mantel seemed to mock her, a constant reminder of the passage of time and the opportunities slipping through her fingers.

Life could be cruel. Fairness, apparently, wasn't guaranteed.

Suddenly, the sharp clang of the Orphanage's bell echoed through the halls, signaling the approach of an unexpected visitor. Charlotte straightened, her heart quickening with a mixture of trepidation and curiosity. Visitors were a rare occurrence, and the staff hurried to tidy the common areas and ensure the children were presentable.

From her vantage point, Charlotte caught a glimpse of an unfamiliar carriage rolling through the iron gates, its polished exterior gleaming in the sunlight. The crest emblazoned on the side caught her eye, and she leaned forward, straining to make out the details. Who could be calling upon the Orphanage, and what could they want?

Chapter Two

The clatter of hooves and the creak of carriage wheels disrupted the usual quiet of the Hawthornfield Orphanage. Charlotte's heart fluttered with curiosity. Visitors were rare at the orphanage, especially in the middle of the day.

The carriage was unlike anything she had seen before - its polished mahogany panels gleaming in the weak winter sun, the team of matched bays pulling it with an air of importance. As the coach drew closer, the children paused in their tasks, whispering hurriedly to one another. Even the ever-vigilant Mrs. Higgins appeared at the doorway, her thin lips pursed in an unreadable expression.

The carriage came to a stop, and the driver leapt down to open the door. Charlotte's breath caught as an elderly gentleman emerged, his movements slow and deliberate. He was dressed impeccably in a black frock coat and waistcoat, a gold pocket watch glinting at his waistline. His hair, gone mostly to silver, was neatly combed, and a pair of round spectacles perched on the bridge of his nose.

This man, with his air of confidence and refinement, seemed utterly out of place amongst the drab, institutional walls of the orphanage. As he turned his gaze upon the courtyard, the children fell silent, their previous chatter replaced by a hush of anticipation.

Mrs. Higgins hurried forward, her skirts rustling, to greet the visitor. "Mr. Pembroke," she said, dipping into a shallow curtsy. "This is an unexpected pleasure. To what do we owe the honour of your visit?"

Mr. Pembroke's lips curved into a polite smile as he inclined his head. "Good day, Mrs. Higgins. I'm afraid I've come on a matter of some importance." His gaze swept over the children, and Charlotte felt a jolt of unease, as if those keen eyes had singled her out amongst the group.

"Of course, sir. Please, allow me to show you to my office." Mrs. Higgins gestured towards the imposing double doors that led deeper into the orphanage. "Children, back to your duties," she called sharply, her eyes narrowing as she noticed their stares.

Reluctantly, the children resumed their tasks, but Charlotte couldn't tear her gaze away from the retreating figures of Mrs. Higgins and Mr. Pembroke. What business could this distinguished-looking gentleman have with the orphanage? And why did she feel a growing sense of both trepidation and anticipation at his arrival?

Mr. Pembroke's footsteps echoed against the bare, scrubbed floors as he followed Mrs. Higgins through the orphanage's corridors. The air here was thick with the reek of disinfectant, a stark contrast to the crisp, fresh outdoors he had just left behind.

His lips tightened imperceptibly as he took in the grim, joyless atmosphere - the high ceilings, the drab walls, the lack of any personal touches or signs of child's play. This was no place for young, curious minds to thrive, he mused.

As they passed by a group of children diligently scrubbing the floorboards, Mr. Pembroke's gaze briefly settled on one girl in particular. She stood out from the others, her movements more precise, her expression one of quiet contemplation rather than the dull resignation he saw on the faces around her.

Their eyes met for the briefest of moments, and Mr. Pembroke felt a stirring of recognition. There was a spark in this girl, a glimmer of potential that the dreary confines of this institution seemed intent on snuffing out.

He quickly averted his gaze, however, as Mrs. Higgins glanced back at him, her brows furrowed in a mixture of deference and unease. "This way, Mr. Pembroke," she murmured, ushering him through a set of heavy wooden doors.

The matron's office was just as joyless as the rest of the orphanage, its sole decorations a crucifix and a portrait of the Queen. Mr.

Pembroke took a seat in the chair she indicated, folding his hands in his lap as Mrs. Higgins settled behind her desk.

"Now, sir, how may I be of assistance?" she asked, her voice clipped and formal.

Mr. Pembroke drew a slow breath, his gaze sweeping the room once more before settling on the woman before him. "I've come to discuss a matter of some importance, Mrs. Higgins," he began, his tone measured. "It concerns a particular child here at your institution."

The heavy oak door to Mrs. Higgins's office was cracked open just a sliver, allowing snatches of the conversation within to drift out into the dimly lit corridor.

"A particular child, you say?" Mrs. Higgins's voice, laced with skepticism, carried through the gap. "Pray tell, Mr. Pembroke, to which child are you referring?"

A pause, then the measured tones of the elderly gentleman. "I've come to speak with you about a young girl I believe has great potential. A girl who, with the proper guidance, could achieve remarkable things."

Charlotte, crouched just out of sight, strained to hear more. Her heart pounded in her chest as she waited with bated breath for Mrs. Higgins's response.

"Potential?" The matron's voice dripped with disdain. "These children are here to learn practical skills, Mr. Pembroke, not to indulge in fanciful dreams. We must prepare them for a life of service, not... not flights of fancy."

Another pause, weighted with tension. "I understand your concerns, Mrs. Higgins. But I assure you, this girl's talents lie in a far more tangible realm than mere flights of fancy."

Charlotte unconsciously leaned closer, her eyes wide with a mixture of hope and trepidation. What was Mr. Pembroke proposing? And why did the idea make her pulse quicken with anticipation?

Mrs. Higgins's response was curt. "I'm afraid I cannot simply allow you to spirit away one of my charges, Mr. Pembroke. These children are under my care, and I have a responsibility to see that they receive a proper upbringing."

"I'm not asking you to 'spirit away' anyone, Mrs. Higgins." Mr. Pembroke's tone remained calm, but a hint of steel had crept into his words. "I'm simply requesting the opportunity to... assess this young girl's abilities. To determine if she might benefit from a different sort of guidance than what you can provide here."

Charlotte's breath caught in her throat as the implications of his words sank in. Could this be her chance - her chance to escape the stifling confines of the orphanage and explore the world beyond? Her fingers curled into the fabric of her skirt, knuckles whitening with the force of her grip.

Mrs. Higgins let out a huff of disapproval. "I'm not sure I feel comfortable with that, Mr. Pembroke." She looked down at her lap, then back up, eyes relaxed somewhat. These children are my responsibility, and I will not simply hand them over to the first well-to-do gentleman who comes calling."

The sound of a chair scraping against the floor reached Charlotte's ears, and she shrank back, heart racing. Had she been discovered?

Mr. Pembroke's gaze swept the room again as he shifted in his seat, and his eyes settled on a small, metal clockwork figure sitting on the corner of Mrs. Higgins's desk. He leaned forward, reaching out to gently pick it up, his weathered fingers moving with a surprising deftness.

The little mechanical man stood just a few inches tall, its limbs articulated to move in a jerky, lifelike manner. As Mr. Pembroke wound the tiny key at its back, the figure began to dance in his palm, the movements smooth and precise.

A faint crease appeared between his brows as he examined the device more closely. The craftsmanship was exquisite, far beyond what one might expect from the crude, mass-produced toys typically found in an institution such as this. There was a level of intricacy and care in its construction that spoke of a keen, inquisitive mind.

Slowly, Mr. Pembroke's gaze drifted back to Mrs. Higgins, who watched him warily. "This is quite an impressive little automaton," he murmured, his voice tinged with a subtle note of approval. "May I ask where it came from?"

Mrs. Higgins's lips tightened into a thin line. "One of the children made it, as part of their lessons. We find it important to teach them practical skills, you understand."

Mr. Pembroke nodded, his fingers tracing the delicate gears and springs of the tiny figure. "Impressive indeed. May I inquire as to which child constructed this?"

The matron hesitated, her eyes narrowing. "I'm afraid I don't recall the specific child responsible. The work is done anonymously, you see, to ensure the children focus on developing their abilities, not seeking praise."

For a moment, Mr. Pembroke's gaze seemed to pierce right through her, and Mrs. Higgins suppressed the urge to fidget under his scrutiny. Then, the elderly gentleman's lips curved into a faint, knowing smile.

"I see." He gently set the automaton back on the desk, his movements almost reverential. "Well, Mrs. Higgins, I must say that the level of craftsmanship displayed here is truly remarkable. Whoever created this has a keen eye for detail and a natural aptitude for mechanics."

His gaze flickered towards the door, as if he could sense the presence of the curious young girl just beyond. "It would be a shame to see such talent go to waste, don't you agree?"

Mrs. Higgins's expression hardened, and she clasped her hands tightly on the desk. "Mr. Pembroke, I understand your interest, but I must insist that the children here receive a proper education, focused on practical skills and obedience. Indulging in... fanciful pursuits is not part of my mandate."

Charlotte's heart pounded in her ears as the sound of footsteps approached the cracked door. She quickly shrank back, pressing herself against the wall, hoping to remain unseen.

The door creaked open, and Mr. Pembroke's measured gaze swept the dimly lit corridor. His eyes settled on the small, huddled figure, and a faint smile tugged at the corners of his lips.

"There you are, my dear," he said, his voice low and gentle. "I had a feeling I might find you here."

Charlotte froze, her eyes wide with a mix of trepidation and curiosity. Slowly, she rose to her feet, clutching the hem of her plain dress.

"I... I'm sorry, sir," she stammered, her gaze averted. "I didn't mean to eavesdrop, I just—"

Mr. Pembroke raised a hand, silencing her. "There's no need to apologize, child. In fact, I'm rather glad you were listening."

Charlotte blinked, her brow furrowing in confusion. "Listening, sir?"

The elderly gentleman chuckled softly. "Yes, my dear. You see, I've come here with a proposition for you, and I believe it's one you may find quite intriguing."

Cautiously, Charlotte lifted her gaze to meet his, her fingers tightening their grip on her dress. "A proposition, sir?"

Mr. Pembroke nodded, his expression earnest. "I couldn't help but notice the remarkable craftsmanship of that little automaton in Mrs. Higgins's office. And I suspect the talented individual responsible for its creation is none other than you."

Charlotte's eyes widened, and she felt a flush of heat rise to her cheeks. "I... I don't know what you mean, sir. I'm just—"

"Now, now, there's no need to be shy," Mr. Pembroke interjected gently. "I can see the spark of intelligence in your eyes, my dear. You have a gift, a natural aptitude for mechanics that I believe deserves to be nurtured and cultivated."

He took a step closer, his gaze warm and encouraging. "I'm an engineer myself, you see, and I've spent a lifetime surrounded by the wonders of machinery and invention. And I believe you, Charlotte, have the potential to follow in my footsteps."

Charlotte's breath caught in her throat, her heart racing. How did this man know her name? And what did he mean, to follow in his footsteps? Was he truly suggesting—

"I'd like to offer you the opportunity to come and work with me, Charlotte," Mr. Pembroke continued, his voice tinged with a note of excitement. "To learn the art of engineering, to hone your skills, and to unlock the full extent of your remarkable abilities."

Charlotte stared at him, her mind reeling. This was all too much to take in, too impossible to be real. Surely, this was just another cruel dream, another fantasy that would be snatched away before she could grasp it.

"But... but why?" she stammered, her voice barely above a whisper. "Why would you want to help someone like me?"

Mr. Pembroke's expression softened, and he reached out to gently touch her shoulder. "Because, my dear Charlotte, I see the potential in you. And I believe that with the right guidance, you can achieve things that will astound even yourself."

Charlotte felt a lump rise in her throat, and she fought to keep the tears of hope and disbelief from spilling down her cheeks. Could this really be her chance to escape the bleak confines of the orphanage and pursue her dreams?

Sensing her hesitation, Mr. Pembroke gave her shoulder a gentle squeeze. "Think it over, my dear. I'll be staying in the area for the next few days, and I'd be more than happy to discuss this further with you. What do you say?"

Charlotte nodded, her voice trembling slightly. "I... I would be honored, sir."

Mr. Pembroke's eyes twinkled with approval, and he offered her a warm smile. "Excellent. Then I shall look forward to our next conversation, Charlotte."

With that, he turned and made his way back down the corridor, leaving the young girl alone with her swirling thoughts and the glimmer of hope that had been ignited within her.

Charlotte stood frozen in the dimly lit corridor, her mind racing as Mr. Pembroke's words echoed in her ears. The idea of leaving the orphanage, of pursuing her fascination with mechanics, was both exhilarating and terrifying.

For years, she had resigned herself to the rigid routine and austere existence of Hawthornfield, burying her dreams beneath the burden of obedience and practicality that Mrs. Higgins demanded. The orphanage had become a cage, its walls closing in around her, stifling her curiosity and ambitions.

Yet, the prospect of escaping those confines and venturing out into the unknown was a daunting one. What if this was all just a cruel illusion, another false promise snatched away before she could grasp it? The thought of having her hopes dashed once more filled her with a sense of trepidation.

Charlotte's gaze fell to her calloused hands, the same hands that had assembled the intricate automaton Mr. Pembroke had admired. She had always taken pride in her mechanical aptitude, but it was a skill she had carefully hidden, fearful of drawing the matron's ire.

Now, this stranger — this Mr. Pembroke — had seen her talent and recognized its potential. The idea that someone, a respected engineer no less, believed she could achieve remarkable things was both exhilarating and overwhelming.

Charlotte's fingers trembled as she considered the opportunity before her. To work alongside Mr. Pembroke, to learn the art of engineering, was a dream she had scarcely dared to entertain. The orphanage had stripped her of so many dreams, and she had grown accustomed to the bitter taste of disappointment.

Yet, there was a glimmer of hope flickering to life within her, a spark that threatened to ignite into a flame of possibility. What if, for once, her dreams were not destined to be crushed underfoot? What if this was her chance to break free from the confines of Hawthornfield and forge her own path?

The fear of failure still lingered, a nagging voice in the back of her mind that whispered of the risks and uncertainties that lay ahead. But as Charlotte recalled the warmth and sincerity in Mr. Pembroke's gaze, a tentative courage began to take root.

Perhaps, just perhaps, this was her chance to seize control of her own destiny, to become more than just another nameless orphan lost in the dreary halls of Hawthornfield. The prospect filled her with a mixture of trepidation and anticipation, a whirlwind of emotions she had scarcely known.

Steeling her resolve, Charlotte took a deep breath and turned, her steps quickening as she made her way back to Mrs. Higgins's office. She knew her decision would not be an easy one, but for the first time in her life, she felt a glimmer of hope that her future might not be as bleak as she had once believed.

Chapter Three

Charlotte stood before Sarah, her hands twisting the hem of her apron nervously. The world beyond the orphanage walls beckoned, but the prospect of leaving her dear friend weighed heavily on her heart.

"So, you're really going?" Sarah's voice was laced with a mix of sadness and resignation.

Charlotte nodded, her eyes downcast. "Mr. Pembroke has offered me the chance to become his apprentice. I... I can't pass that up, Sarah. It's everything I've ever dreamed of."

Sarah reached out and squeezed Charlotte's hand, a bittersweet smile playing on her lips. "I know, Lottie. You deserve this opportunity more than anyone." She paused, her gaze searching Charlotte's face. "You'll do amazing things, I'm sure of it."

The unspoken words hung in the air between them - the acknowledgment of the distance that would soon separate them, the uncertainty of whether their paths would cross again.

Charlotte felt a lump in her throat as she met Sarah's eyes. "I'll miss you, Sarah. You've been the best friend I could have ever hoped for." She pulled her friend into a tight embrace, savoring the warmth and familiarity one last time.

Sarah returned the hug, her own eyes glistening with unshed tears. "Promise me you'll write, Lottie. Promise me you won't forget about this place, or about me."

"I promise," Charlotte whispered, her voice thick with emotion. "You'll always be in my heart, Sarah. No matter where I go."

Charlotte's heart raced as she gathered her few possessions into a small satchel. The worn fabric and faded colors were a stark contrast to the grand opportunity that lay before her. She paused, running her fingers along the well-worn cover of a book – a precious gift from Sarah that had provided solace and inspiration during her darkest days in the orphanage.

Clutching the book to her chest, Charlotte took one last look around the sparse room she had called home for the past eleven years. The barren walls and narrow bed seemed to mock the future that awaited her. Despite the familiarity of this place, she could not help but feel a flutter of excitement at the prospect of leaving.

A sharp rap at the door startled Charlotte, and she quickly tucked the book into her satchel as Mrs. Higgins swept into the room, her austere expression firmly in place.

"So, the day has finally come," the matron said, her tone clipped and devoid of warmth. "I must say, I never thought I'd see the day when one of my charges would be plucked from this institution."

Charlotte straightened her shoulders, determined not to let Mrs. Higgins' disdain dampen her spirits. "Thank you, ma'am, for taking me in all these years," she replied, her voice steady.

Mrs. Higgins' lips thinned into a tight line. "Yes, well, don't go thinking this has been some grand act of charity. You were a useful pair of hands, nothing more." She paused, her gaze sweeping over Charlotte's modest bundle. "Although, I suppose even you managed to prove yourself worthy of better prospects."

Charlotte blinked, taken aback by the unexpected glimmer of respect in Mrs. Higgins' words. Before she could respond, the matron continued, her expression hardening once more.

"Just remember, girl, the world out there is a cruel, unforgiving place. Don't come crawling back here when you realize you're in over your head." With that, Mrs. Higgins turned on her heel and strode out of the room, leaving Charlotte to ponder her parting words.

Charlotte took one last longing look at the Hawthornfield Orphanage, its imposing grey walls a stark contrast to the bustling streets that now surrounded her outside. Gone were the rigid echoes of Mrs. Higgins' voice and the pervasive scent of lye and disinfectant. Instead, the air was filled with the clamour of horse-drawn carriages, the laughter of passersby, and the inviting aromas of distant bakeries.

Clutching her small satchel, Charlotte turned to face Mr. Pembroke, who stood waiting beside his carriage. The older man offered her an encouraging nod, his kind eyes twinkling behind his spectacles.

"Are you ready, my dear?" he asked gently.

Charlotte took a deep breath and nodded, a nervous but determined smile playing on her lips. "Yes, sir. I am."

As the carriage rolled through the lively streets, Charlotte couldn't help but press her face against the window, her eyes wide with wonder. The grand townhouses and bustling shops were a far cry from the monochrome existence she had known within the orphanage walls. People of all stations hurried by, their clothing and demeanour a dizzying array of styles and personalities.

Before long, they slowed to a stop, and Mr. Pembroke gestured towards an elegant, if somewhat weathered, expansive townhouse. "Here we are, my dear – your new home."

Charlotte followed him up the steps, her heart hammering in her chest. The door opened to reveal a spacious foyer, the air thick with the scent of beeswax and old books. She drank in her surroundings, noting the ornate mouldings and the gleam of polished wood. She then followed Mr. Pembroke through the elegant foyer, her gaze darting from the gleaming brass fittings to the intricate wallpaper that adorned the walls.

Mr. Pembroke led her down a corridor, his footsteps muffled by the plush carpet underfoot. "As you can see, my dear, this is a modest but comfortable home," he said, glancing back at Charlotte with a warm smile.

Stepping through an arched doorway, they entered a sprawling room, the walls lined with towering bookshelves. Charlotte's eyes widened as she took in the space – it was a library, filled with volumes on every conceivable subject. Her fingers itched to pull the books from the shelves and lose herself in their pages.

"Feel free to explore the library at your leisure," Mr. Pembroke said, a hint of amusement in his voice as he observed Charlotte's fascination. "But first, let me show you the heart of this household."

He guided her down a long hall, then through another doorway. Then Charlotte's breath caught in her throat, and her eyes widened as Mr. Pembroke pushed open a set of heavy oak doors, revealing a vast, airy space beyond. Sunlight streamed in through tall windows, casting a warm glow over the intricate mechanisms that filled the room.

They had entered a vast, well-lit workshop, its walls adorned with an array of gleaming tools and mechanical parts. Intricate machinery hummed and whirred, the air thick with the scent of oil and metal.

Charlotte's eyes darted from one corner to the next, taking in the ordered chaos that surrounded her. Workbenches were cluttered with half-finished projects, sketches, and ledgers, and Charlotte could practically feel the creativity and innovation pulsing through the space.

"This, my dear Charlotte, is where the real magic happens," Mr. Pembroke said, gesturing proudly around the workshop. "It is here that I, and soon you, will bring our ideas to life. This portion of the building is rather large. Lots of . . . fun, I admit, to be had here. I made sure it could meet my every need."

Charlotte turned to him, her eyes shining with a mixture of wonder and trepidation. "I... I don't know what to say, sir. This is all so overwhelming."

Mr. Pembroke placed a gentle hand on her shoulder. "I understand, my dear. But I see a spark in you – a thirst for knowledge and a boundless curiosity. That is precisely what I need in an apprentice."

Shelves upon shelves of gleaming tools and intricate mechanisms lined the walls, and a massive workbench dominated the centre of the room. Dazzled by the sensory overload, Charlotte could barely contain her excitement.

Mr. Pembroke cleared his throat, a warm smile spreading across his face. "Welcome to your new domain, my dear."

Hesitantly, Charlotte reached out to trace the smooth curve of a gear, her fingers itching to disassemble and reassemble the intricate mechanisms before her. The weight of the metal, the precision of the craftsmanship – it all spoke to her in a language she had only just begun to understand.

"Remarkable, isn't it?" Mr. Pembroke murmured, his keen eyes watching her every move. "This is where I spend most of my days, tinkering and experimenting." He chuckled softly. "I daresay you'll be spending quite a bit of time here as well, my dear."

Charlotte looked up at him, her eyes shining with a mixture of wonder and trepidation. "I... I don't know what to say, sir. It's all so..." She paused, searching for the right words. "It's so different from the orphanage. So *alive*."

Mr. Pembroke nodded, his expression softening. "Indeed it is, my dear. And I have a feeling you're going to fit right in." He gestured towards a workbench in the corner, where a partially disassembled pocket watch lay. "Now, why don't you take a look at that and see what you can make of it?"

Eagerly, Charlotte approached the workbench, her fingers gently caressing the delicate parts. As she began to meticulously examine each component, a sense of focus and determination washed over her, and the rest of the world faded away. This was her element, her true calling – and she was determined to prove herself worthy of Mr. Pembroke's faith in her.

Charlotte's fingers danced across the delicate mechanisms of the pocket watch, her brow furrowed in concentration. The rhythmic ticking filled the air, a soothing cadence that allowed her to lose herself in the task at hand.

"Quite the natural, aren't you, my dear?"

Charlotte's head snapped up at the sound of Mr. Pembroke's voice, a flush creeping up her cheeks. "I-I'm sorry, sir. I didn't mean to get so absorbed. I was just—"

Mr. Pembroke raised a hand, his weathered features softening into a warm smile. "No need to apologize, my dear. In fact, I'm delighted to see you so engrossed." He stepped closer, his gaze filled with a paternal pride that caught Charlotte off guard.

"You have a remarkable gift, Charlotte," he continued, "and I'm honored to have the chance to nurture it." Clasping his hands behind his back, he began to slowly pace the length of the workbench, his eyes scanning the various tools and parts.

"You see, when I first laid eyes on you at the orphanage, I knew there was something special about you. A spark, a curiosity that set you apart from the rest." He paused, his gaze meeting Charlotte's. "And now, seeing you at work, I'm more certain than ever that you have the makings of a truly exceptional engineer."

Charlotte felt a flutter of excitement in her chest, but beneath it, a familiar twinge of uncertainty lingered. "But, sir, I'm just an orphan. How could I possibly—"

"Ah, but you underestimate yourself, my dear." Mr. Pembroke interjected, his voice gentle yet firm. "Your humble beginnings do not define you. What matters is the passion and determination that burns within you." He moved closer, placing a weathered hand on her shoulder.

"I see in you the same drive and resourcefulness that once propelled me. And I believe, with the proper guidance and education, you can achieve greatness." His eyes twinkled with a hint of mischief. "After all, what is an engineer if not a dreamer who dares to turn their vision into reality?"

The weight of Mr. Pembroke's words settled over Charlotte, a profound sense of possibility unfurling within her. Gone was the timid orphan, replaced by a young woman who dared to imagine a future beyond the bleak confines of Hawthornfield.

"I... I don't know what to say, sir," she murmured, her voice barely above a whisper.

Mr. Pembroke chuckled warmly. "Then don't say anything, my dear. Simply embrace the opportunity before you."

He paused, his expression turning contemplative. "Although, there is one more matter I wish to discuss with you."

Charlotte felt her heart skip a beat, a flutter of apprehension fluttering in her chest. Had she done something wrong already? Had she somehow disappointed the man who had so generously plucked her from the orphanage?

Mr. Pembroke seemed to sense her unease, for he quickly reached out and gave her hand a gentle squeeze. "Fear not, my dear. This is nothing to be concerned about."

He gestured towards a pair of ornate armchairs in the corner of the workshop. "Why don't we have a seat? I believe this conversation will be best had in a more comfortable setting."

Charlotte followed him, her mind racing with a thousand unanswered questions. As they settled into the chairs, Mr. Pembroke fixed her with a serious yet kind gaze.

"Charlotte, as you know, I have taken you under my wing and brought you here to be my apprentice." He paused, his fingers drumming thoughtfully against the arm of his chair. "But what you may not know is that I have come to see you as much more than just an apprentice."

Charlotte felt her breath catch in her throat, her heart pounding in her ears. Was he about to send her away? Surely, she couldn't have disappointed him so soon.

"You see, my dear," Mr. Pembroke continued, his voice soft and measured, "I have come to care for you deeply. You remind me so much of myself at your age – curious, determined, and brimming with untapped potential."

He leaned forward, his gaze never wavering from hers. "And that is why I have decided to make you a most extraordinary offer."

Charlotte held her breath, her fingers gripping the arms of the chair in anticipation.

"Charlotte, I would be honored if you would allow me to formally adopt you as my own." A warm smile spread across his weathered features. "I want to give you a new life, a new name, and a new future beyond the constraints of the orphanage."

The days that followed were a whirlwind of activity and discovery for Charlotte. Each morning, she would eagerly make her way to the workshop, her fingers already itching to delve into the intricate mechanisms that lay waiting.

Under Mr. Pembroke's assistant's watchful eye, Charlotte had been formally named Charlotte Pembroke, losing the surname assigned to her at the orphanage, a transition that still felt foreign on her tongue. But the kind, matronly housekeeper—Henrietta Clarke—had a way of putting her at ease, guiding her through the nuances of her new life with a gentle patience.

"You know, Miss Charlotte," Henrietta would say, her spectacles perched on the end of her nose as she oversaw Charlotte's work, "Mr. Pembroke has spoken very highly of you. He sees great things in your future, mark my words."

Charlotte would feel a flush of pride at the older woman's words, her hands steadying as she continued her task. Though she missed the familiar comfort of Sarah's companionship, Henrietta had become a steadfast and reassuring presence in her life.

In the quiet moments, Charlotte would retreat to her room, the weight of her new name and responsibilities weighing heavily on her. Carefully, she would pull out a worn, leather-bound journal and began to pen a letter to her dear friend.

"My dearest Sarah," she would write, her words flowing freely, "I wish I could convey to you the wonders I have witnessed in this place. The workshop is a veritable wonderland of gears and gadgets, and Mr. Pembroke has been most generous in sharing his knowledge with me."

She would pause, the nib of her pen hovering over the paper as she contemplated the right words. "I miss you terribly, my friend. The halls of this grand estate, though filled with the hum of industry, can seem so lonely without your familiar laughter to fill them."

Occasionally, a stray tear would land on the page, blurring the ink, but Charlotte would quickly blink them away, determined not to let her emotions overwhelm her.

"I promise to write to you as often as I can, dearest Sarah. And I hope, one day, you will be able to see this place for yourself. Until then, know that you are always in my thoughts."

Then she would carefully fold the letter, sealing it with a small, homemade wax seal before tucking it away, ready to be entrusted to the next courier bound for the orphanage.

Charlotte soon found herself settling into a comfortable routine. The workshop had become a sanctuary, a place where she could lose herself in her passion. Though Mr. Pembroke was often away on business the first or two, his presence lingered in the carefully curated tools and half-finished projects that surrounded her.

And when the elderly engineer did return, Charlotte would find herself drawn to his paternal gaze, eager to share her latest accomplishments and hear the stories of his travels. It was in these moments that she truly felt at home, her heart swelling with a sense of belonging that she had never known in the cold, impersonal halls of the orphanage. It was then she would truly start her journey into her apprenticeship.

The rhythmic ticking of the pocket watch filled the air as Charlotte's nimble fingers danced across the delicate mechanisms. Brow furrowed in concentration, she meticulously examined each component, her mind racing with the possibilities.

It had been just over a month since Mr. Pembroke had brought her to his grand estate, and Charlotte found herself immersed in a whirlwind of new experiences. Gone now were the drab, institutional confines of the orphanage, replaced by the warm, industrious atmosphere of the workshop. Where the orphanage had stifled her natural curiosity, this newfound home nurtured it, pushing her to explore the wonders of engineering and mechanics.

Under Mr. Pembroke's patient tutelage, Charlotte's understanding of the intricate world of machinery slowly unfolded. He would sit with her for hours, guiding her through the fundamentals, his weathered hands demonstrating the precise movements required to assemble and disassemble the various components.

"You see, my dear," he would say, his voice soft yet authoritative, "the key is to approach each task with a keen eye and a steady hand. Rushing leads to mistakes, and mistakes can have costly consequences. And of course, unhappy customers."

Charlotte would nod, her eyes fixed on his every word, committing each lesson to memory. Where once she had felt overwhelmed by the sheer complexity of the workshop, she now found herself navigating the space with growing confidence.

The repetition of the tasks, once daunting, became a soothing rhythm – the gentle tapping of her tools, the faint hiss of steam, and the satisfying click as each piece fell into place. It was as if the machines were speaking to her, revealing their secrets one by one.

And with each new skill she mastered, Charlotte felt a surge of empowerment coursing through her. Gone was the timid orphan, replaced by a young woman who dared to dream of a future beyond the constraints of her past.

"Remarkable, my dear," Mr. Pembroke would murmur, a proud smile tugging at the corners of his mouth as he observed her work. "You have a true gift for this."

Charlotte would feel a flush of pride at his words, her heart swelling with a sense of belonging she had never experienced before. This was her domain now – a place where her talents were not only recognized but celebrated.

One such day, as she worked, her gaze happened to drift towards a neatly stacked pile of papers on the corner of the workbench. Curiosity piqued, she reached out and gently sifted through them, her eyes scanning the neat, flowing script.

Most of the documents appeared to be old letters, their edges yellowed and delicate. Charlotte's heart skipped a beat as she noticed one particular envelope, its wax seal still partially intact. Carefully, she slid her finger beneath the flap, the paper crackling softly as she unfolded the letter within.

The words seemed to jump off the page, their meaning slowly unraveling in Charlotte's mind. She read and re-read the elegant script, her breath catching in her throat as she pieced together the implications.

Charlotte's eyes scanned the letter once more, her heart pounding in her ears. The words seemed to jump off the page, their meaning slowly unraveling in her mind.

"...but as an orphaned child in your care, whether now or when she's older..." and "may not be stated as such, but we both understand he would have considered you an option…"

Charlotte's breath caught in her throat. Could it be possible? Was she the one they spoke of? Surely not. Yet, the wording stirred something deep within her, a glimmer of hope that perhaps, just perhaps, there was more to her story than she had ever known.

Her gaze shifted to the signature at the bottom of the letter - a name she did not recognize. An attorney. Gently, Charlotte folded the letter, her fingers trembling slightly. Should she say anything?

Charlotte glanced around the workshop, half-expecting Mr. Pembroke to materialize and catch her prying into his affairs. But the room was quiet, save for the steady ticking of the pocket watch she had been repairing. Carefully, she placed the letter back atop the stack, her heart heavy with unanswered questions.

As she resumed her work, Charlotte's mind raced, fitting the pieces together like the delicate mechanisms before her. Could it be that her humble beginnings were not as simple as she had been led to believe? The prospect both thrilled and terrified her.

Charlotte's fingers stilled, and she found herself staring at the pocket watch, its rhythmic ticking a soothing counterpoint to the turmoil within her. In that moment, she made a silent vow to herself - she would not confront Mr. Pembroke until she was certain she was ready to hear whatever secrets he might hold. For now, she would focus on her work, on honing the skills that had brought her to this remarkable place.

With a deep breath, Charlotte set her shoulders and returned to the task at hand, her brow furrowed in concentration.

As she leaned in, squinting at the stubborn piece before her, a sudden knock at the door startled her, and for a moment her own guilt made her check the stack of letters, as if some might had made their way into her pockets unbidden. Moments later, Henrietta Clarke entered, a tray of tea and biscuits in her hands.

"Ah, there you are, Miss Charlotte," the housekeeper said, her kind eyes crinkling in a warm smile. "I thought you might be in need of a little refreshment."

Charlotte returned the smile, though it felt strained. "Thank you, Henrietta. That's very thoughtful of you."

As Henrietta bustled about, pouring the steaming tea, Charlotte's gaze drifted back to the stack of letters, her mind still consumed by the revelations they had uncovered.

The mystery would just have to wait.

As late winter became early summer, Charlotte's fascination with the workshop only grew. She would lose herself in the intricate schematics, her fingers tracing the delicate lines as she imagined the mechanisms coming to life. And when she successfully completed a project, the surge of accomplishment was unlike anything she had ever felt. He'd called her a prodigy. She didn't know about that, but she knew she lived for nothing else. Maybe that's what a prodigy was. The others treated her nice, almost like a colleague. At first. She could tell some in his employ didn't like the preferential treatment she received. They were nice enough, for the most part. But the younger apprentices closer to her age eyed her askance when they thought she wouldn't notice. But she did.

Yet Charlotte made sure to balance her learning with down time. Even she needed time away to collect herself. His home —*her* home, now—provided plenty of that. Plenty of time, and plenty to visit.

The expansive gardens of the Pembroke estate quickly became Charlotte's sanctuary, a verdant oasis where she could escape the occasional bustle of the workshop. Owning—and connecting—the townhomes on either side gave him one of the largest estates this side of town. He could have had more, but he wanted the perfect blend of country and city both. So he'd made it, being the wealthy eclectic he was.

So on warm afternoons, she would wander the winding paths of the gardens behind, her fingers tracing the delicate petals of blooming roses or the rough bark of ancient oaks. The peaceful tranquility offered a welcome respite from the rhythmic hum of machinery, allowing her mind to roam freely.

One day, as she meandered through the carefully manicured hedgerows, she stumbled upon a secluded alcove – a small, wrought-iron gazebo nestled amidst a tangle of climbing vines. Stepping inside, Charlotte felt a sense of wonder wash over her. The dappled sunlight filtered through the leaves, casting a warm, golden glow over the space. Sinking into the weathered bench, she allowed her mind to drift, the gentle breeze caressing her face.

It was in moments like these that Charlotte felt the weight of her choice – the decision to leave the only life she had ever known. The orphanage, for all its austerity, had been a familiar constant, a place where she had learned to navigate the rigid confines of her existence. But now, surrounded by the boundless possibilities of the Pembroke estate, she found herself grappling with a newfound sense of freedom.

As she traced the intricate patterns of the wrought-iron, Charlotte's thoughts drifted to Sarah, her dearest friend. She could almost hear the other girl's laughter echoing through the halls of the orphanage, a sound she now found herself longing for. In the quiet solitude of the gazebo, she reached into the pocket of her dress, pulling out a carefully folded letter. With a wistful sigh, she began to pen another missive, her words flowing with a bittersweet mix of joy and nostalgia.

"My dearest Sarah," she wrote, "I find myself overwhelmed by the vastness of this new world I now inhabit. The workshop, with all its wonders, is a place I have come to cherish, but even it pales in comparison to the beauty that surrounds me here."

She paused, her brow furrowing slightly. "Yet, for all the freedom I have been granted, there are moments when I find myself yearning for the familiar comforts of our shared room, and the sound of your voice echoing through the halls."

Charlotte's fingers trembled slightly as she continued, the weight of her decision settling heavily on her heart. "I hope you can understand, my friend, that while my affection for you has not wavered, I have found a place where my talents can truly flourish. But I promise, I shall never forget the bond we share, nor the memories we have made."

Carefully folding the letter, Charlotte pressed a gentle kiss to the paper before tucking it safely away. As she rose from the bench, she cast one last, lingering gaze around the secluded alcove, a bittersweet smile playing on her lips.

Many months had now passed since Charlotte had arrived at the Pembroke estate, and the initial whirlwind of new experiences had begun to settle into a comfortable routine. The workshop remained her sanctuary, a place where she could lose herself in the intricate world of machinery and engineering. But the vast expanses of the estate had also become a canvas for her inquisitive nature, each nook and cranny a potential treasure trove waiting to be explored.

As Charlotte lay in the comfort of her bed, the faint sounds of outside lulling her towards sleep, she found herself reflecting on the journey that had brought her here. The orphanage, with its stark halls and rigid structure, now seemed like a distant memory, a life she had shed like an old, ill-fitting coat. In its place, she had been welcomed into the warm embrace of the Pembroke household, something she had never dared to dream of.

Closing her eyes, Charlotte allowed the weight of her decision to settle over her. The freedom and opportunities that now lay before her were both exhilarating and daunting. Gone were the constraints of the orphanage, replaced by a world of endless possibilities. And with that came the responsibility of forging her own path, of proving herself worthy of the trust Mr. Pembroke had placed in her.

But even as she grappled with the gravity of her new circumstances, Charlotte couldn't help but feel a profound sense of gratitude. The loneliness and uncertainty that had once haunted her days had been replaced by a growing sense of belonging, a realization that she was no longer just an orphan, but the cherished ward of a man who saw the potential in her. He was now her adopted father.

Family.

With a contented sigh, Charlotte allowed her thoughts to drift, her mind slowly succumbing to the gentle pull of sleep. Tomorrow, she knew, would bring new challenges and adventures, but in this moment, she felt a profound sense of peace. For the first time in her life, she was truly home.

Chapter Four

As the seasons shifted and the days grew longer, Charlotte's life at the Pembroke estate settled into a steady rhythm. Each morning, she would awake to the soft chimes of the grandfather clock, the familiar sound rousing her from slumber. With a gentle smile, she would rise and make her way to the workshop, the promise of new discoveries spurring her onward.

The workshop itself had become a sanctuary, a place where time seemed to stand still. Charlotte would lose herself for hours, her nimble fingers deftly navigating the delicate mechanisms of the various contraptions that filled the space. Mr. Pembroke would often join her, offering guidance and encouragement as she honed her skills, her passion for engineering growing with each passing day. He was open, and wanted those who worked—and apprenticed—with him to feel at home there. Many would come and go as their schedules allowed. Some who were students came sporadically, others, the more seasoned employees of his, worked regular hours.

Charlotte was now a trusted, new apprentice, her hands deftly navigating the intricate workings of the various contraptions that filled the workshop. Mr. Pembroke's faith in her had only grown stronger with time, and he often marveled at the depth of her understanding, her ability to solve complex problems with an almost intuitive ease.

One morning, as Charlotte stood before a partially disassembled steam engine, lost in contemplation, Mr. Pembroke approached her, a thoughtful expression on his weathered face.

"Charlotte, might I have a word?"

She turned, her eyes shining with curiosity. "Of course."

Mr. Pembroke cleared his throat, his gaze steady. "I've been giving some thought to the future, my dear, and I believe it's time we discussed your path forward."

Charlotte felt her heart skip a beat, a flicker of apprehension crossing her features. "My path forward, sir?"

"Yes," he said, placing a gentle hand on her shoulder. "You've shown remarkable aptitude and dedication to your work here, and I believe it's time to consider the next steps in your development as an engineer."

An engineer? Charlotte nodded, her fingers stilling on the engine's intricate mechanisms. "I am prepared to discuss my future, sir."

Mr. Pembroke's lips curved in a faint smile. "Excellent. As you know, I have a meeting with some potential investors in London rapidly approaching, and I've been entrusted with showcasing some of our most innovative designs. I believe the time has come for you to take on a more prominent role in our work here."

Charlotte's eyes widened, her heart swelling with pride and a touch of trepidation. "You mean... to work on the pieces they'll be seeing?"

"Precisely," Pembroke said, his gaze warm. "I've been most impressed by your progress, my dear. Your keen mind and skillful hands have earned you this opportunity."

He turned, walking her over towards a workbench where several intricate schematics were laid out. "Now, let me show you the designs we've been developing. I believe your input will be invaluable."

He wants my input!

As Pembroke began to explain the various components and mechanisms, Charlotte felt a thrill of anticipation. This was her chance to truly make her mark, to prove herself worthy of Pembroke's trust.

Beside them, the workshop's other occupants paused in their work, their gazes turning towards Charlotte and Pembroke with a mixture of curiosity and respect. Among them was a young man named Thomas, whose brow furrowed slightly as he watched the exchange. He'd been kind and always polite, but dismissive at the same time, and Charlotte had trouble figuring him out.

She imagined, to Thomas' chagrin, this newcomer - an orphan girl - had been entrusted with a task of great import. He probably couldn't help but wonder how this would impact his own standing and future within the workshop, a realm in which he was still establishing his foothold following Pembroke's decision to unite all his endeavours under one roof.

Sensing the shift in the room, Pembroke glanced up, his expression mildly reproachful. "Ah, Thomas. I see you've been observing our discussion. Come, join us. I believe Charlotte could benefit from your insights on the steam-powered loom."

Thomas hesitated, then nodded, moving to stand beside them, his gaze flickering between Pembroke and Charlotte with a complex mix of emotions.

Charlotte's heart raced with excitement as Pembroke outlined the intricacies of the designs. This was her moment, her chance to demonstrate the full extent of her abilities. No longer would she be seen as merely an orphan girl – here, in this bustling workshop, she would forge her own path as a skilled engineer.

Brow furrowed in concentration, Charlotte listened intently, her nimble fingers instinctively reaching out to trace the delicate schematics. Pembroke's faith in her had not been misplaced; she was determined to prove herself worthy of the trust he had placed in her.

However, as the discussion continued, Charlotte couldn't help but notice the subtle shift in the atmosphere. While Pembroke spoke enthusiastically of her involvement, the other men in the workshop – including Thomas, Pembroke's longtime apprentice, unlike her – regarded her with a mixture of skepticism and unease.

One of the engineers, a Mr. Wilkins, cleared his throat and stepped forward. "Forgive me, Mr. Pembroke, but is it wise to entrust such an important project to a mere girl? Surely one of us more experienced hands would be better suited to the task."

Charlotte felt her cheeks flush at the dismissive words, but she kept her expression neutral, waiting for Pembroke's response. Though they must surely know she was also his adopted daughter, the men in the workshop still seemed to doubt her abilities. She steadied her breathing, determined not to let their condescension unsettle her.

Pembroke's brow furrowed, a flash of displeasure crossing his features. "Mr. Wilkins, I can assure you that Charlotte's skills are more than equal to the challenge. She has proven herself time and time again in this very workshop."

"But, sir, she is still so young," Wilkins pressed, his gaze flickering to Charlotte with a hint of condescension. "Surely there are more practical concerns we must consider before entrusting her with such an important endeavour."

Charlotte could feel the weight of the men's sceptical eyes upon her, but she straightened her shoulders, determined not to show any sign of weakness. She would prove her worth, no matter their doubts.

Charlotte stood tall, her jaw set with determination, as Pembroke's weathered gaze swept over the assembled men.

"Gentlemen, I understand your concerns, but I can assure you that Charlotte's abilities are more than equal to the task at hand." His voice was firm, brooking no argument. "She has shown remarkable aptitude and dedication to her work, and I have the utmost faith in her capabilities."

Pembroke placed a reassuring hand on Charlotte's shoulder, his expression softening. "Now, let us return to the designs and hear Charlotte's thoughts. I'm certain she has some valuable insights to share."

Turning his attention back to the schematics, Pembroke began to explain the intricate workings of the steam-powered loom in greater detail, pausing periodically to gauge Charlotte's reactions and ask for her input.

When she spoke, her voice was clear and confident, her suggestions both practical and innovative. The other men, once hesitant, soon found themselves drawn into the discussion, their initial reservations giving way to genuine interest.

Pembroke beamed with pride, his gaze filled with a warm, paternal affection. "Excellent, my dear. I knew your insights would be invaluable."

Later, as the others returned to their tasks, Pembroke gestured for Charlotte to follow him to a quieter corner of the workshop.

"Charlotte," he said, his voice low and sincere, "I want you to know that I have the utmost faith in your abilities. You have worked tirelessly and proven yourself time and again. Do not let the doubts of others shake your confidence."

He reached out, gently cupping her chin and tilting her face up to meet his gaze. "You are a gifted engineer, my dear, and I am honored to have you as my apprentice. Remember that, no matter what challenges may arise."

Charlotte felt a lump rise in her throat, overwhelmed by the depth of Pembroke's belief in her. "Thank you, sir," she said, her voice barely above a whisper. "I will not let you down."

Pembroke smiled, his eyes crinkling at the corners. "I know you won't, my dear. Now, let us return to the work at hand. There is much to be done if we are to dazzle the future backers of our work."

Charlotte nodded, her spirits lifted, and followed Pembroke back to the bustling workshop, her determination renewed.

Days turned into weeks as Charlotte immersed herself in the design and construction of the improved loom for the upcoming pitch. At times, the challenges seemed insurmountable, the delicate components frustratingly uncooperative. But Charlotte refused to be deterred, her resilience and quick thinking helping her navigate each obstacle.

One particularly vexing issue arose with the loom's gear system, which refused to engage properly. Charlotte spent hours tinkering and adjusting, her hands growing callused from the long days of meticulous work. Just when she was about to admit defeat, a flash of inspiration struck, and she devised a ingenious solution that had the gears meshing smoothly.

Pembroke, who had been observing Charlotte's progress, beamed with pride. "Excellent work, my dear!" he exclaimed, placing a weathered hand on her shoulder. "I knew you had it in you."

Charlotte felt a surge of elation, her cheeks flushed with the thrill of her triumph. For once, the doubting glances of the other men in the workshop were nowhere to be seen – they had all gathered around, their expressions a mix of awe and newfound respect.

Even Thomas, who had initially regarded Charlotte with thinly veiled resentment when he thought he could get away with it, now watched her with a newfound appreciation. As she demonstrated the loom's flawless operation, he found himself impressed by her ingenuity and technical prowess.

Yet, the road to success was not without its setbacks. On another occasion, Charlotte encountered a vexing issue with the steam engine's pressure valve, which threatened to derail the entire project. Frustrated and exhausted, she spent long hours poring over diagrams and experimenting with various solutions, her hands growing blistered from the heat of the engine.

Just as she was about to give in to despair, Pembroke approached her, his wise eyes filled with understanding. "My dear, you've been working tirelessly. Perhaps it's time to take a short respite, hmm?" He gently guided her away from the engine, suggesting a restorative cup of tea.

Reluctantly, Charlotte agreed, and as she sipped the fragrant brew, she felt her mind begin to clear. With renewed focus, she returned to the engine, and after several more hours of painstaking work, she finally cracked the problem, adjusting the valve with a deft touch.

Pembroke beamed with pride as he watched Charlotte's triumph, her face alight with a sense of accomplishment. "Splendid, my dear!" he exclaimed, placing a hand on her shoulder. "I knew you had it in you."

As she wandered the Pembroke estate one afternoon, the tranquil gardens offered a welcome respite from the intensity of her training as they often did. She still marveled at it all, as if her adoption was only yesterday.

How did I come to be so lucky?

The verdant hedgerows and neatly manicured pathways were a stark contrast to the dreary confines of the Hawthornfield Orphanage, where she had spent her childhood up until only quite recently in her life. Here, the air was filled with the sweet fragrance of blooming flowers, a far cry from the stale, institutional scent of her former home; a home that was still engrained in her senses.

Charlotte paused, gazing up at the grand manor house that loomed before her. Its stately façade, with its ornate windows and intricate brickwork, was a testament to the wealth and prestige of Mr. Pembroke. It was a world away from the bleak, spartan walls of the orphanage, where personal expression and individuality were so often stifled.

A small smile tugged at the corners of her lips as she recalled the ceaseless reprimands of Mrs. Higgins, the stern matron whose disapproving gaze had hounded her every step. The woman had made it abundantly clear that Charlotte's fascination with mechanics was an impractical and unbecoming pursuit for a young lady. How different things were now, with Pembroke not only encouraging her talents but actively entrusting her with important projects.

Charlotte's fingers traced the delicate petals of a nearby rose, her mind drifting to the challenges she had faced in the workshop. The skepticism of the other engineers, their dismissive attitudes towards her abilities, had stung at first. But with Pembroke's steadfast support and her own unwavering determination, she had proven herself time and time again.

Yet, she still fought it. The doubt. She knew she did. Charlotte felt she would forever be proving herself.

As she wandered deeper into the gardens, Charlotte couldn't help but wonder what the future might hold. Would the other men in the workshop ever fully accept her, or would there always be an undercurrent of doubt and resentment? And what of Thomas Keating, Pembroke's longtime apprentice? A peer in age only. They were from completely different lives.

Charlotte's brow furrowed, a sense of unease stirring within her. She couldn't help but notice how Thomas's gaze had grown increasingly guarded in recent weeks, a subtle shift that set her nerves on edge. Try as she might, she couldn't shake the feeling that he harboured some hidden animosity, a resentment that might one day boil over and threaten the fragile balance she had worked so hard to achieve through her own unwavering determination. The thought unsettled her, for she had come so far, overcoming the initial doubts and prejudices of her male counterparts with Pembroke's steadfast support. Now, the prospect of Thomas's growing resentment threatened to undo all that she had built, leaving her once again having to prove her worth in a world that seemed intent on denying her rightful place.

With a deep breath, Charlotte pushed those worries aside, focusing instead on the beauty that surrounded her. For now, she was content to bask in the tranquility of the gardens, her mind already whirring with new ideas and solutions to the challenges that awaited her in the workshop.

Chapter Five

Charlotte, now sixteen years old, moved with practiced ease through the bustling workshop, the familiar sights and sounds as comforting as an old friend. The rhythmic clanging of tools, the hiss of steam, and the occasional muffled curse from the other engineers had become the soundtrack to her days.

With a quick glance at the pocket watch Pembroke had gifted her, Charlotte gathered her coat and hat, eager to make the most of the rare free afternoon Pembroke had granted her. As she stepped out into the crisp autumn air, she couldn't help but revel in the sense of freedom that had become her constant companion since leaving the orphanage behind.

Charlotte made her way to the nearby bakery, the tempting aromas of freshly baked bread and pastries beckoning her inside. The familiar chime of the shop's bell announced her arrival, and the kindly old shopkeeper looked up from her counter, her weathered face breaking into a warm smile.

"Why, if it isn't our young Charlotte!" the woman exclaimed, her voice carrying a lilting lilt. "I was wondering when I'd be seeing you again, my dear."

Charlotte returned the smile, feeling a rush of affection for the friendly shopkeeper. "Good afternoon, Mrs. Wilkins," she greeted, her tone polite yet genuine. "I've been rather busy with work, but I couldn't resist the temptation of your delectable baked goods."

Mrs. Wilkins chuckled, her eyes twinkling with amusement. "Ah, yes, I heard tell you've been working hard, making all sorts of clever contraptions with Mr. Pembroke. Well, you must be in need of a little treat, then." She gestured towards the display of freshly baked pastries. "Go on, my dear, have a look and see what catches your fancy."

Charlotte's gaze swept over the enticing array of flaky croissants, buttery scones, and delicate tarts, her mouth watering with anticipation. There was a time she couldn't imagine such treats. *Nor could I have ever afforded them.* After a moment's deliberation, she selected a few of her favourites, carefully placing them in a small paper bag.

"Thank you, Mrs. Wilkins," she said, handing over the coin Pembroke had entrusted her with. "These will be perfect for my afternoon stroll."

"Ah, yes, enjoy your free time, my dear," the shopkeeper replied, her smile widening as she accepted the payment. "You work so hard, you deserve a little respite now and then."

Charlotte nodded, her expression softening. "I certainly shall," she assured the kind woman, tucking the bag of pastries into the crook of her arm. With a polite farewell, she stepped back out into the crisp autumn air, the familiar scent of the bakery lingering in her nostrils.

As she strode along the crowded thoroughfare, Charlotte couldn't help but feel a profound appreciation for the fleeting instances of contentment that punctuated her daily routine. The kindness of Mrs. Wilkins, the simple pleasure of a freshly baked treat, the freedom to explore the world beyond her home – these were the things that sustained her, that made the long hours of hard work and the occasional challenges she faced all the more bearable.

As Charlotte strolled back towards the Pembroke estate, the familiar sights and sounds of the bustling city streets surrounded her. The crisp autumn air carried the scent of freshly baked bread from the bakery, and the rhythmic clop of horses' hooves on the cobblestones created a soothing cadence. Yet, as she made her way, Charlotte couldn't help but notice a group of girls, no more than ten or twelve years old, laughing and playing in the nearby park.

Charlotte observed the girls in the park, their carefree laughter and playful antics tugging at something deep within her. A bittersweet pang of nostalgia stirred, as she recalled the fleeting moments of happiness from her childhood at the Hawthornfield Orphanage, before the harsh realities of that life had taken hold. She couldn't help but wonder what it would have been like to have a normal upbringing, to experience the joys of play without a care in the world. Charlotte remembered the long hours spent cleaning, scrubbing, and sewing, and while she took immense pride in her work and the mentorship of Mr. Pembroke, there was still a part of her that yearned for the carefree joy she witnessed in the park. But one could not go back to earlier years. And she was content, mostly.

With a quiet sigh, Charlotte turned away, continuing on her path towards the Pembroke estate. The bittersweet pang of nostalgia lingered, a reminder of the childhood she had never truly known. Yet, as she walked, her steps grew more determined, her mind already focused on the tasks that awaited her in the workshop. For Charlotte, the work she did, the machines she tended to, and the inventions she helped create were a source of solace, a way to channel her restless energy and find a sense of purpose.

As she approached the familiar gates of the Pembroke estate, Charlotte couldn't help but feel a sense of gratitude for the life she had found here. *Home.* Her *home.* While it may not have been the idyllic childhood she had once dreamed of, it was a life filled with purpose, challenge, and the occasional moments of joy that she had come to cherish.

With a renewed sense of determination, Charlotte stepped through the gates, her mind already turning to the projects that awaited her. The familiar scent of oil and metal greeted her, and she couldn't help but feel a sense of excitement at the prospect of delving into her work once more.

However her life had started, she'd found her place in the world.

As winter came and went, eventually giving way to the promise of warmer days, Charlotte once more felt the pull of the nearby park and the expansive vista it offered of the bustling city. The manicured grounds and winding paths attracted a veritable tapestry of humanity, a diverse array of individuals representing the many walks of life that thrived in the metropolis. Charlotte found herself drawn to observing these passing figures, mentally cataloguing their appearances and mannerisms, pondering the stories that might lie behind each face, each stride. Mr. Pembroke told her it was the engineer in her; a chance to indulge her innate curiosity about the world beyond her own small sphere of existence.

She paused, once again observing some young girls, again with a more contemplative gaze. Their lives, so vastly different from her own at that age, filled her with a sense of both wonder and longing. How quickly the years seemed to be passing, transforming her from a timid orphan into a capable, self-assured young woman. Life was a strange thing.

With a soft sigh, Charlotte turned away, her feet guiding her back to the grand library within the Pembroke estate. Settling into a plush armchair, she lost herself in the pages of a technical manual, her mind already whirring with ideas and solutions to challenges she hadn't yet faced. On the side table lie novels and fanciful stories she had yet to open, but intended to at some point when her mind was less busy. Some of the men had suggested she read them instead.

But of course they would.

Yet Charlotte was perfectly content to be the best she could be, thank you very much. And that meant study.

Mr. Pembroke paused in the doorway of his workshop, watching Charlotte with a mixture of pride and concern. Her brow furrowed in concentration as she meticulously adjusted the intricate mechanism before her, her skilled fingers moving with a deftness that belied her young age.

At just sixteen years old, Charlotte had blossomed into a capable and passionate apprentice, her natural aptitude for engineering evident in every project she undertook. Pembroke marveled at how far she had come since he had first discovered her tinkering with discarded toys at the Hawthornfield Orphanage.

Yet, as he observed her, a faint crease formed between his brows. While he had no doubt of Charlotte's abilities, he could not ignore the societal obstacles she would inevitably face as a young woman in a field dominated by men. The path ahead would be fraught with challenges, from skepticism to outright disdain, and

Pembroke feared for how she would navigate those treacherous waters.

Especially when I'm not around to help her. But that was a thought best ignored for the time being.

Clearing his throat, he stepped into the workshop, drawing Charlotte's attention. "Excellent work, my dear," he said, his tone warm but tinged with a hint of worry. "I must say, you continue to impress me with your dedication and skill."

Charlotte's face lit up with a proud smile, and Pembroke felt a twinge of guilt for the unease that lingered in the back of his mind. "Thank you," she replied, her voice brimming with enthusiasm. "I've been studying the latest advancements in steam-powered machinery, and I believe I've found a way to improve the efficiency of our-"

As Charlotte launched into a detailed explanation of her latest project, Pembroke listened attentively, his admiration for her intellect and passion growing with every word. Yet, beneath the surface, his concern persisted. He knew that the world beyond the Pembroke estate would not be as welcoming or as accommodating as the workshop he had built.

Pembroke resolved to do all in his power to ensure Charlotte's success and happiness, even if it meant shielding her from the harsh realities she was sure to face. For now, he would continue to nurture her talents and provide her with the resources and support she needed to thrive. He could give plenty of both. But deep down, he knew that the true test lay ahead, and he could only hope that Charlotte's resilience and determination would see her through. *And it won't be long before you discover truths as yet unknown, my dear,* he thought. Had he been wrong to wait? Would she resent him for not telling her sooner? She looked so much like her father…

Charlotte's teeth worried at her bottom lip as she paused outside the workshop door, the muffled voices of Pembroke's associates drifting from the office next door. She had been fetching a tool Pembroke had requested, but now found herself rooted to the spot, unable to pull herself away.

"I just don't see how it's proper for a young lady to be involved in such matters," one voice said, laced with condescension. "Engineering is hardly a fitting pursuit for a woman of good breeding. And what we're doing here? The promises we can make? I mean, really . . . "

Charlotte felt her cheeks flush with indignation. How dare they speak of her in such a way, as if she were some delicate flower incapable of understanding the complexities of machinery. She had worked tirelessly under Pembroke's tutelage, her nimble fingers and keen intellect proving time and again that she was more than capable of holding her own. Many times she fixed what they couldn't!

Another man hummed in agreement. "Hmm, well, Pembroke has always been a bit... unconventional. Taking in that orphan girl—and adopting her, no less—*and* educating her in the ways of machinery. It's simply not done."

Charlotte's heart sank. She had always known that her position here was somewhat unconventional, that Pembroke's decision to take her under his wing and nurture her talents was viewed as unorthodox by many. But to hear it spoken of so dismissively, as if her very existence were an affront to propriety, stung deeply.

Clutching the tool tightly, Charlotte fought the urge to burst through the door and confront the men directly. She knew that would only serve to further cement their low opinion of her. Instead, she took a deep breath, steadying her nerves, and continued on her way, her steps measured and controlled.

As she entered the workshop, Pembroke glanced up from the intricate mechanism he was tinkering with, his weathered face breaking into a warm smile. "Ah, there you are, my dear. I was beginning to wonder what was keeping you."

Charlotte forced a smile in return, handing him the tool. "Forgive me, sir. I... I was momentarily detained." She hesitated, unsure of whether to share what she had overheard, but ultimately decided against it. Pembroke had always been her staunchest advocate, and she didn't wish to burden him with the narrow-minded judgements of his associates.

"No matter," Pembroke said, waving a dismissive hand. "Now, come, let me show you the latest adjustments I've made. I think you'll find them quite fascinating."

As Pembroke launched into an enthusiastic explanation of his work, Charlotte allowed herself to be drawn back into the familiar rhythms of the work, the voices from the hallway fading into the background. Here, surrounded by the familiar sights and sounds of machinery, she felt at home, her doubts and insecurities momentarily forgotten.

But deep down, a seed of uncertainty had been planted. Charlotte couldn't help but wonder how many others shared the views of Pembroke's associates, and whether the path she had chosen would continue to be met with such resistance. Still, she was determined to prove them wrong, to show that a woman could indeed excel in the field of engineering.

Yet as days turned into weeks following that conversation, she began to encounter more overt resistance from some of the older, more traditional engineers.

During meetings, they would cast doubtful glances in her direction, muttering under their breath about the impropriety of a woman pursuing such a masculine profession. One particularly bold engineer even had the audacity to suggest that Charlotte would be better suited to more "feminine" pursuits, such as sewing or embroidery.

At first, the engineers had likely found her presence novel, even endearing—a young girl in their male-dominated world. But as she had grown in both stature and ability, their amusement had given way to something else entirely.

She was there to stay, and clearly they didn't like it.

Threatened by her intellect and skill, the older men now regarded her with thinly veiled disdain. Their comments, though never directly aimed at her, stung all the same. Charlotte could sense their discomfort, their unease at the prospect of a woman encroaching on their territory; but not just any woman, one clearly with Pembroke's favour.

Despite the mounting resistance, Charlotte remained steadfast in her determination. She knew her worth, her capabilities, and she refused to be cowed by the narrow-minded opinions of those who refused to see her as an equal. Pembroke had faith in her, and that was all that mattered.

As she meticulously adjusted the gears in front of her, Charlotte caught the eye of one of the older engineers, a man whose perpetual frown and gruff demeanor had earned him the nickname "Grumbles" among the apprentices. Their gazes locked, and for a moment, Charlotte thought she saw a flicker of begrudging respect in his weathered features.

But just as quickly, the expression was gone, replaced by a dismissive snort as he turned away. Charlotte felt her jaw tighten, the urge to confront him rising like a wave within her. How dare he look down on her, as if her very presence were an affront to his sensibilities?

Before she could act, however, Pembroke's gentle voice broke the tension. "Charlotte, my dear, would you be so kind as to assist me with this delicate adjustment?" he asked, his eyes searching her face with a mixture of pride and concern.

Forcing herself to take a deep breath, Charlotte nodded and moved to Pembroke's side, her hands steady and her focus unwavering. She would not let the narrow-mindedness of a few old men deter her.

Charlotte's cheeks burned with indignation, but she refused to let their words rattle her. Instead, she redoubled her efforts, tackling each new challenge with unwavering determination. She would prove her worth through her actions, not by engaging in petty arguments.

Still, the constant barrage of skepticism and condescension began to wear on her, chipping away at the confidence she had built under Pembroke's tutelage. She found herself second-guessing her abilities, wondering if perhaps the others were right – that she simply didn't belong in this world of gears and machinery.

They'd rather have me back at the orphanage, no doubt, she thought. *Back to the clueless girl they think I am.*

Frustrated and disheartened, Charlotte finally confided in Pembroke about the challenges she was facing. The older man listened intently, his brow furrowing with concern.

"I must admit, my dear, that I had feared you would encounter such resistance," he said, his voice tinged with regret. "The path you have chosen is not an easy one, even for the most capable of individuals."

Pembroke sighed heavily, removing his spectacles and polishing them with the edge of his waistcoat. "The unfortunate truth is that society has certain expectations of women, and engineering is not often seen as a suitable pursuit. But I have never doubted your abilities, Charlotte, and I will not allow these narrow-minded fools to deter you."

He reached across the desk, grasping her hand in his weathered one. "You have a gift, my dear, a keen mind and an unwavering determination that I have rarely seen in one so young. Do not let the doubts of others sway you from your path. Trust in yourself, and know that I will always be in your corner. You are, after all, my adopted daughter as well. Never forget who you are."

Charlotte felt a swell of emotion rise within her, and she squeezed Pembroke's hand in return, gratefully.

With a renewed sense of purpose, Charlotte threw herself back into her studies, tackling increasingly complex projects with a fervor that astonished even Pembroke. The day would come when she would silence her critics, and she would do it through the sheer force of her abilities.

Chapter Six

The rhythmic clang of tools filled the workshop as Charlotte worked then tightened the last bolt, her brow furrowed in concentration. At seventeen, she had grown into a more confident and capable apprentice, taking on increasingly complex tasks under Pembroke's watchful eye.

Just last week, Pembroke had entrusted her with overseeing the installation of a new boiler system, a testament to the trust he had placed in her abilities. The memory of the older engineers' disapproving glances still stung, but Charlotte refused to let their petty resentment deter her. She would prove her worth through her work, one step at a time.

As she wiped the grease from her hands, Charlotte's gaze drifted to the framed letter that sat on the workbench, the familiar looping script of her dear friend Sarah greeting her. The two had kept up a steady correspondence since Charlotte's departure from the orphanage, and the letters always brought a bittersweet pang of nostalgia.

I wish you could see all that I've accomplished, Sarah, she thought, tracing the elegant lines of the ink with her fingertip. *If only you could be here to share in this adventure.*

A soft clearing of the throat interrupted Charlotte's reverie, and she turned to find Pembroke standing in the doorway, his weathered face etched with an uncharacteristic solemnity.

"Charlotte, my dear, might I have a word?" he asked, his voice tinged with a subtle hint of weariness.

Sensing the gravity in his tone, Charlotte nodded and followed him to the cozy confines of his office, where the familiar scent of old books and pipe tobacco enveloped her. Pembroke gestured to the chair across from his desk, and Charlotte perched on the edge, her heart beginning to race with unease.

"Is something wrong, sir?" she asked, her voice barely above a whisper, a faint hint of concern lacing her words.

Pembroke let out a heavy sigh, his gaze trained on the smouldering embers in the fireplace, the flickering light casting shadows across his weathered features. "I'm afraid there is, my dear. It's my health. I... I've been keeping something from you, and I feel it is only right that I share it with you now." His brow furrowed, a subtle tension creeping into his expression as he prepared to broach the delicate subject.

Charlotte felt a chill crawl down her spine as she watched the flickering flames dance, casting shadows across Pembroke's face. Whatever he was about to say, she knew it would change everything.

Pembroke drummed his fingers on the arm of his chair. How was he going to tell his young protégée about this? He had grown to care for her like a daughter, and this weighed on him, especially since he had so little time left. It wasn't unexpected, but it was sooner than he had hoped.

He had first noticed the signs weeks ago – the occasional dizziness, the fatigue that seemed to come from nowhere. At first, he had told himself it was because of the long hours he'd been putting in, but as the symptoms continued, he couldn't ignore the truth.

He looked at the stacks of blueprints and sketches in the corner of his office. The heart of his life. This was his life's work, the machine that could change everything, and he had put so much into it. And now he might not live to see it through. He needed to get it in order, especially now. And now that his time might be limited, it made him realize the task he needed to complete. And then if he couldn't do it, who would?

That was the penultimate question.

His gaze settled on Charlotte, who sat across from him, her brow creased with concerned curiosity. She had come so far, blossoming from the shy, uncertain child he had plucked from the orphanage into a driven, talented young woman. Pembroke knew that she possessed the brilliance and the determination to bring his dreams to fruition, but the thought of burdening her with such a weighty responsibility filled him with a profound sense of unease.

"Charlotte," he began, his voice tinged with a rare vulnerability, "I'm afraid I have not been entirely forthcoming with you. You see, I... I've been experiencing some health issues of late." He paused, watching the concern deepen in her expression. "The doctors have informed me that my condition is quite serious, and that I . . . well,

I may not have much time left. And although they can't say with certainty, I may also live a long life yet." He shrugged. "Frustrating, really. Not to know one way or the other, although it feels obvious to me, at least. But, it's important that you, my daughter in nearly every sense of the word, knows."

Pembroke's heart ached at the sight of the anguish that flickered across Charlotte's face, the realization of what his words meant slowly sinking in. He reached across the desk, his weathered hand grasping hers in a gesture of comfort and reassurance.

"Now," he said, his expression softening with a hint of a sad smile, "how about a nice supper in town, just you and I? We can discuss a few things. This will need time to sink in, for both of us. And some time together away from all this would be nice."

Later that night, Charlotte lay awake in her bed, the flickering lamplight casting shadows across the familiar contours of her room. Pembroke's grave words still echoed in her mind, the weight of his revelation bearing down upon her like a heavy shroud.

A lump formed in her throat as she thought of the man who had taken her in, nurtured her dreams, and become a true father figure. The idea that he might not have much time left was almost too much for her to bear. Her heart ached with a profound sense of loss and uncertainty.

Yet, as Charlotte replayed their conversation, she recalled how Pembroke had insisted they carry on as if nothing were amiss. He had spoken of the unpredictability of his condition, reminding her that the doctors could not say for certain. Charlotte knew he was trying to spare her from needless worry, to maintain a sense of normalcy in the face of this unsettling news.

With a deep, steadying breath, Charlotte resolved to do just that. Pembroke had entrusted her with so much, had believed in her when no one else would. The least she could do was honor his wishes and continue on as they always had - with unwavering determination and a commitment to their shared passion for engineering.

As she closed her eyes, the memory of their shared supper in town came to the forefront of her mind. Pembroke had been his usual self, guiding their conversation with his trademark blend of wisdom and warmth. Together, they had discussed nearly anything and everything. It had been a welcome respite from the heaviness of their earlier discussion, a chance to reconnect and find comfort in their familiar routine.

The next week, with newfound curiosity about things, Charlotte found herself drawn to the cluttered workbench in the corner of Pembroke's office, the one he kept locked most of the time, her fingers tracing the worn edges of a stack of papers that had caught her eye. It wasn't like Pembroke to leave his papers in such disarray – the man was meticulous in his organization, each blueprint and sketch carefully filed away. These were scattered inside the top box, corners sticking out.

Looking over her shoulder, Charlotte carefully lifted the topmost papers and gently pulled, her eyes widening as she recognized the intricate diagrams and technical schematics. These were nothing like anything she had seen among Pembroke's usual projects, the designs far more complex and unfamiliar.

Her heart began to race as she studied the pages, a growing sense of curiosity mingling with a slight unease. What was the nature of this mysterious project that Pembroke had kept hidden from her all this time? Surely, as his most trusted apprentice, she would have been privy to such an ambitious undertaking.

Carefully, Charlotte sorted through the documents, her brow furrowing in concentration as she pieced together fragments of information. Mentions of "Project Arcanum" and cryptic references to "groundbreaking electromagnetic advancements" piqued her interest, kindling a spark of determination within her.

She needed to know more. Pembroke's recent revelation about his declining health had only strengthened Charlotte's resolve to honor his legacy and see his life's work to completion. If this secret project held such significance, then it was her duty to uncover its mysteries and ensure that Pembroke's vision came to fruition, even if he could not see it through himself.

Charlotte looked around the workshop again and set to work sorting the papers, making sure not to disturb the order. As she did so, she brushed her fingers against a leather-bound journal. She picked it up and opened it.

As she read the first few lines of Pembroke's personal notes, a picture began to form in her mind. Pembroke had a personal connection to this "Project Arcanum," one that went back to his youth. It seemed to be a longtime, albeit lofty dream of his. This project was important to him, and Charlotte felt she owed it to him to figure out what it was.

She worked quickly, cataloging each scrap of paper and every sketch, and thinking about what she had just discovered. Whatever it was that Pembroke had been hiding, Charlotte was determined to find out.

Pembroke had watched with a faint smile hidden by the doorway as Charlotte carefully sorted through his scattered documents, her brow furrowed in concentration. He had deliberately left them in plain sight, knowing full well that her curious nature would draw her to investigate.

Truth was, he'd been meaning to tell her about Project Arcanum for a while now. He'd been in poor health for a while now, maybe a smidge longer than he'd hinted to her, and the weight of this unfinished business had grown more pressing on his mind. Charlotte, his most trusted protégée, his adopted daughter, deserved to know.

Before the week was out, he and Charlotte were taking supper in the cozy dining room. Pembroke cleared his throat, catching Charlotte's attention.

"My dear, I couldn't help but notice you've been going through the papers on... well, something important to me. My pet project, a love of mine. 'Project Arcanum.' I didn't know how or when I should bring this up." He smiled slightly. "I'm sorry to bring it up like this, I really had intended to talk to you about it."

Charlotte's eyes widened slightly, a little fear crossing her face. "I... I didn't mean to pry, sir. I was simply curious about what this project was. I'm sorry, I shouldn't have-"

Pembroke held up a hand. "No, you should. In fact, I'm glad you did. The truth is, Project Arcanum is what I've been working on for my entire life, a passion that has driven me for decades."

He paused, looked out the window where the sun was setting and casting a warm glow over everything. "You see, this project actually started in a significant moment of my life, one that changed everything for me. It was a time of great excitement, but also of great loss and heartbreak. Others . . . had shared in the vision with me. Only a theory, at the time. But I've come closer to realization. My . . . friend, would have loved to see where it's going."

Charlotte listened intently, her fingers trembling slightly as she clasped her teacup. She had never seen this pensive, vulnerable side of Pembroke before, and it stirred a sense of unease within her.

"I've kept the details of this project closely guarded, even from those closest to me. Yes, money would flow in if I . . . Well. This could revolutionize the world." Pembroke's eyes met Charlotte's, a silent plea for understanding shining in their depths. "Perhaps I'm being a bit pedantic. But well, now, with my health failing, I feel it is time to entrust you with the truth. You, Charlotte, have become like a daughter to me, and I want nothing but openness between us. Can I tell you about it?"

That night, as Charlotte lay in her bed, the weight of her conversation with Pembroke hung heavy on her mind. She stared up at the ceiling, the flickering candlelight casting dancing shadows across the plain walls of her room.

Pembroke's admission that his work was deeply personal had brought up a lot of questions for Charlotte. He had told her a lot about his childhood, his early education… But it only raised more questions. He hadn't told her much about what he wanted to do with this project he hardly ever visited. She got the sense he wanted to tell her, but he hadn't.

Maybe he's waiting to see if he's going to die before he tells me everything, she thought, her brow furrowing. Pembroke's health had been declining, and Charlotte knew he was probably coming to terms with the fact that he didn't have much time left. The thought of losing him filled her with a deep, aching dread.

She was going to have to read further into the documents and sketches she had found. He hadn't said no. And if this project meant so much to him, then she had to do whatever she could to make sure it was completed, even if he couldn't do it himself.

But where did he stand on it? He had been clear she was going to inherit almost everything. That had been quite the shock, and the main reason for taking her out that night at dinner. Maybe he wanted her to put her talents elsewhere and leave his special project be. She wanted to ask but didn't want to be insensitive. *So you just snoop,* she thought, chiding herself.

He was clearly a brilliant man ahead of his time. But to what end? Although he'd said himself it wasn't *what* he was working towards as much as why: and that why was about leaving the world a better place. Then he'd told her she embodied the same curiosity for life as he had. And he wanted her life to hold whatever meaning she wanted to give it. As an orphan in an orphanage, she could never have had that chance without resources. So his project was important, he'd said, but it was more about his relationship with her.

The project was also way beyond her current understanding of energy and mechanics. Thus, it enthralled her all the more. Terms like *free energy,* and notes and equations about *magnetic fields.* These were far outside of what they did there in his home. And yet, he often repeated to all his associates and apprentices his favourite saying with a twinkle in his eye: *A focused mind is an accomplishing mind. But a mind kept from dreams accomplishes nothing.*

As she read some the documents he freely shared, Charlotte began to notice hints and clues that intrigued her. Pembroke's notes referred to some significant discovery from his past that seemed to be the key to understanding more about Project Arcanum.

But before she could delve deeper, a sudden and severe decline in Pembroke's health brought Charlotte's investigation to a halt. The news of her mentor's rapidly deteriorating condition filled her with a deep, overwhelming sense of dread. All thoughts of the project were pushed aside as she focused her attention on supporting Pembroke during this difficult time. The whole house did, and Charlotte was the front of it alongside Henrietta.

Days passed and she knew it was near. She would soon be on her own again, without the warm presence of the man she'd grown to think of as not just her father in the eyes of the law, but her father in truth.

As she sat by his bedside, holding his weathered hand in her own, Charlotte's heart ached with the realization that she may lose him much sooner than she was ready for. And she suspected there were things he knew about her past that might die with him. So much yet she didn't know! And it pained her in addition to his approaching passing. The weight of his unfinished legacy, coupled with the uncertainty of her own origins, threatened to consume her. She was more determined than ever to honor Pembroke's life's work, but the ticking clock of his declining health only added to the sense of urgency and emotional investment that gripped her.

In the quiet moments by his side, Charlotte found herself whispering a silent prayer, begging for the chance to learn the full story before it was too late. More than that, she begged him to remain on earth as long as the good Lord allowed. She'd grown to love him as he had her.

But she feared his time was at hand.

You've been the only real family I've known...

As the days went, so too, the nights. He deteriorated rapidly, and it wasn't much longer before Pembroke left her world. His passing left Charlotte devastated, the weight of her loss compounded by the unfinished legacy he had entrusted to her.

In the frantic days that followed, she found solace in the familiar, sitting in his favourite chair for hours, walking the same route he loved most... Henrietta, Pembroke's steadfast housekeeper and Charlotte's oftentimes maternal figure, lingered close by, her weathered face etched with concern. She placed a gentle hand on Charlotte's arm, her touch conveying the unspoken comfort of a lifetime spent tending to the needs of this household. Though her own grief was palpable, Henrietta remained a pillar of strength, offering Charlotte a sympathetic ear should she need to give voice to the tempest of emotions swirling within.

A week or so later—time seemed to pass unnoticed, now—Charlotte sat in the familiar comfort of Pembroke's office and personal workshop. Her fingers lightly carressing the worn edges of the workbench, a gesture that had become a source of solace in the days since his passing.

Henrietta's soft footsteps drew her attention, and Charlotte looked up to see the kind-faced housekeeper offering her a steaming cup of tea. "Thought you might be needing this, my dear," Henrietta murmured, her voice tinged with the same quiet sorrow that had cloaked the household since Pembroke's death.

Charlotte accepted the cup gratefully, savoring the warmth that seeped into her hands. "Thank you, Henrietta. I... I don't know what I'd do without you here." Her voice wavered slightly, the words laced with a deep, aching grief.

Henrietta settled into the chair beside her, her own eyes glistening with unshed tears. "Richard was a fine man, and he thought the world of you, Charlotte. We both did." She reached out, giving Charlotte's hand a gentle squeeze. "He spoke of you often, you know - how proud he was of your talents, and how he saw himself in your curious nature."

Charlotte nodded, swallowing past the lump in her throat. "He meant everything to me. I can't imagine a life without his guidance, his unwavering belief in me." She paused, her gaze drifting to the shelves that housed his meticulously organized collection of blueprints and sketches. "And now, with this... this personal project of his, I feel as if I've only begun to unravel the depths of his brilliance."

Henrietta's expression softened with understanding. "Aye," she sighed, "the dear man kept that project close to his heart. I remember the day you arrived here, all those years ago - he was positively bursting with excitement, as if he knew you were the one to carry on his work." She chuckled softly, the sound tinged with bittersweet nostalgia. "You should have seen the look on his face when he realized just how gifted you were with those gears and machines."

Charlotte couldn't help but smile at the memory, the warmth of Henrietta's words soothing the ache in her heart. "I'll never forget that day, Henrietta. I was so terrified, leaving the only life I'd ever known. But Mr. Pembroke... he had a way of making me feel at home, even in the midst of such uncertainty." She paused, her gaze turning pensive.

Before Henrietta could respond, the sound of the door connected to the house opening drew their attention. Charlotte's heart skipped a beat as she recognized the family solicitor, Mr. Ainsley, striding into the workshop, his expression solemn.

"Miss Pembroke," he began, his voice carrying a note of gravity, "I'm afraid I have some important matters to discuss with you, regarding Mr. Pembroke's estate."

Charlotte felt a flutter of apprehension, but Henrietta's steady presence beside her provided a subtle reassurance. "Of course, Mr. Ainsley. Please, sit down. Or would you like to go to his office?"

The solicitor shook his head and cleared his throat, producing a thick envelope from his briefcase. "It seems Mr. Pembroke has made... rather extensive provisions in his will. As his protégée and the one he entrusted with carrying on his life's work, he has named you the sole heir to both his workshop and his home."

Charlotte's eyes widened in surprise, the teacup trembling in her grasp. "I... I don't understand. His home? Everything? Meaning even the workshop here? His business?" She turned to Henrietta, searching the housekeeper's face for any sign of shock or disbelief, but found only a quiet acceptance.

"It's true, my dear," Henrietta murmured, her weathered hand reaching out to still Charlotte's. "Mr. Pembroke thought the world of you. He wanted to ensure that his legacy would live on through you, and that you would have the means to continue your work without hindrance. Of course, he wanted us all to remain here in support of his home. You'll have help as he did. Especially in the affairs of his business, isn't that right Mr. Ainsley?"

The weight of Pembroke's trust and generosity settled upon Charlotte's shoulders, a profound sense of responsibility mingling with her grief. She swallowed hard, her gaze meeting Mr. Ainsley's. "Then... I accept. I will do everything in my power to honor his memory and see his dreams realized."

As the solicitor outlined the legal details in the days that followed, Charlotte found herself navigating a whirlwind of paperwork and meetings, all the while grappling with the enormity of the task that had been entrusted to her. Henrietta's steady presence at her side provided a much-needed anchor, the housekeeper's decades of experience within the Pembroke household proving invaluable.

Together, they ensured that the workshop remained a hub of activity, with Charlotte overseeing the day-to-day operations and the employees who had served Pembroke faithfully. It was a lot to process, but she did her best. For him.

Chapter Seven

She was utterly exhausted. Two weeks since his passing and Charlotte felt like she was punishing herself, drowning in her own self-doubt. But what choice did she have? Pembroke had taken her in, trusted her. Loved her, even. He'd said so himself the night he passed. Who was she, after all? A nobody. But he hadn't thought so, and that was what mattered. Charlotte needed to earn the trust he'd put in her, a trust she felt she didn't deserve in the first place. That meant finishing the work he hadn't, no matter the cost.

And that meant his pet project. He'd wanted it done.

What was the nature of this mysterious project that had consumed her mentor's passion and ingenuity? The designs before her—and more importantly his notes—hinted at revolutionary breakthroughs, yet their purpose remained stubbornly elusive. Far above her capabilities, at least for now. But she didn't back down from challenges. Charlotte's heart raced with a combination of excitement and trepidation. She had always relished a challenge, but the stakes had never been so high.

Pembroke had entrusted her with this monumental task, and she would not – could not – let him down. Swallowing the lump that had formed in her throat, Charlotte steeled her resolve. She would unravel the secrets of it, no matter how daunting the task might be. Even the name Arcanum itself meant *mystery.* How perfect.

Surveying the cluttered study, Charlotte's gaze settled on the armchair where Pembroke had often sat, deep in thought, puffing contentedly on his pipe. A wave of melancholy washed over her, and she could almost hear his comforting baritone, offering words of encouragement and guidance.

"I won't let you down, Mr. Pembroke," she murmured, her fingers tightening around the edge of the drafting table. "I'll see this through, for you and for the future you envisioned."

Yet the weeks that followed, Charlotte felt utterly adrift without Mr. Pembroke's steady presence guiding her every step. The grand estate, once a beacon of promise and possibility, now seemed an endless maze of towering bookshelves and echoing hallways. Her mentor's absence left a gaping chasm, and Charlotte found herself struggling to navigate the transition on her own.

It was Henrietta, the ever-vigilant housekeeper, who became Charlotte's steadfast anchor in the days that followed. The matronly woman, with her sharp eyes and no-nonsense demeanor, made it her personal mission to ensure Charlotte's well-being. She would materialize at Charlotte's side, a tray of warm tea in hand, whenever the young engineer found herself faltering. When she wasn't doing that, Charlotte found it amusing she seemed to be closer to the cook's side more often than not, and she was surprised she hadn't noticed the affection between the two before. It was endearing.

"Now then, my dear," Henrietta would say, her voice soft yet unwavering. "You must keep up your strength. Mr. Pembroke would have it no other way."

Charlotte would nod mutely, gratefully accepting the offer of companionship. In Henrietta's presence, the tightness in her chest eased, and she could almost imagine Pembroke's kind eyes crinkling with a reassuring smile.

Slowly, the household staff – a few trusted individuals who had dedicated their lives to serving the Pembroke estate – began to take Charlotte under their collective wing. The cook was a kindly gentleman with a generous heart, and he would always ensure an extra portion of hearty stew or freshly baked bread found its way to Charlotte's plate at mealtimes. The gardener, a gruff but good-natured fellow, took the young girl under his tutelage, teaching her the ways of tending to the estate's verdant gardens. Charlotte found solace in these small acts of kindness, the simple pleasures of good food and the beauty of nature soothing her troubled soul in the days that followed Pembroke's passing.

It was in these moments, over a bowl of stew or while tending to the garden, that Charlotte began to feel a sense of belonging. The estate was a well-oiled machine, and the routine of it, the familiarity of it, was a balm to her. The sound of the garden shears, the smell of the kitchen, the sound of the staff, it all lulled her in a way she had not been lulled since Pembroke's passing. In these moments, she could almost forget the responsibility that now lay on her shoulders, the responsibility to continue Pembroke's work, to discover the secrets of his life's work. She could simply be, if only for a few moments.

One evening, as Charlotte sat in the cozy kitchen, Henrietta bustling about and the cook's assistant humming a soft melody, she allowed herself a moment of respite. "There you are, my dear," Henrietta said, placing a steaming mug of tea before Charlotte. "Drink up, now. You've been working yourself to the bone, and it won't do. Mr. Pembroke would have my hide if I let you waste away."

Charlotte managed a small smile, wrapping her fingers around the familiar warmth of the mug. "Thank you, Henrietta. You are a rare treasure, no doubt, to us all."

The housekeeper tsked, tutting affectionately. "Nonsense, child. We're family, and that's what families do. Now, drink up and get some rest. The work will still be there in the morning."

For a fleeting moment, she felt a sense of peace wash over her. This was her home now, as surely as the orphanage had been. And with Henrietta and the loyal staff by her side, Charlotte knew she could face whatever direction her life would take next.

Yet the puzzle remained: He had something that was important to him, and she owed him her life. It was a heavy, although pleasing, burden.

She was in over her head with his work, but could never admit it. Not to the others, at least. At least not initially.

One afternoon, Charlotte finally gathered the courage to consult the workshop's senior technicians, hoping they might shed some light on questions she had. She approached the group cautiously, her hands clasped tightly before her.

"Excuse me, gentlemen," she began, her voice soft but unwavering. "I was hoping you could assist me with a matter of some importance."

The men turned to her, their expressions ranging from curiosity to skepticism. Charlotte steeled herself, aware of the lingering doubts about her abilities as a female engineer.

"It's regarding Mr. Pembroke's, uh, personal project – the one he was working on before..." She paused, swallowing the lump in her throat. "I'm afraid I'm having trouble comprehending some of the more technical details. I was hoping you might be able to offer some insight."

The men exchanged glances, and one of the older technicians, a gruff-looking fellow with a thick beard, stepped forward.

"Miss Pembroke," he said, his tone gruff but not unkind. "We're all aware of your mentor's...project. But the truth is, the designs are unlike anything we've ever seen. The principles involved are quite complex, even for the most seasoned of us. Truthfully . . . well. There's not much to be said. He wasn't exactly forthcoming with it. It's what he did in his own time. Away from his business in London. Either way," he said, looking at her over his glasses, "I'm not sure what you can do for it. If we couldn't."

Charlotte's heart sank, and she felt the familiar stirrings of self-doubt. But before she could respond, Henrietta strode into the workshop, her sharp eyes landing on the group.

"There you are, my dear," the housekeeper said, her stern facade crumbling to reveal a soft, maternal warmth. "I thought I might find you here, tormenting these poor men with your endless questions."

The technicians chuckled, some of the tension in the air dissipating. Henrietta turned to them, her hands planted firmly on her hips.

"Now, you lot, I know Mr. Pembroke's project is a puzzle, but I'll not have you undermining the girl's confidence. She's the brightest, most determined young thing I've ever laid eyes on, and if anyone can make sense of those designs, it'll be her."

Charlotte felt a surge of gratitude and renewed determination as Henrietta's unwavering faith washed over her. Squaring her shoulders, she met the technicians' gazes with a newfound resolve.

"I appreciate your honesty, gentlemen," she said. "But I assure you, I am more than capable of unraveling something from his work. Now, with your guidance, I am confident I can make sense of even the most complex principles involved."

The men exchanged surprised glances, and the gruff technician nodded slowly.

"Very well, Miss Pembroke. We'll do what we can to assist you. But be warned – this is no easy task you've set for yourself. He was eclectic. You know that. Out there at times. He left us to pay the bills with the work he couldn't handle, but never seemed to share the passion project that you know more about than us. This," he said, gesturing to the various components strewn about, "was in never-ending supply. Kept us working. *Keeps* us working. His business. But he trusted you to whatever he trusted you with, and frankly, he seemed to think you capable."

Charlotte offered them a determined smile, her eyes alight with purpose.

"I'm not one to shy away from a challenge," she replied. "But other eyes are always needed."

And so it went. As Charlotte's 18th birthday approached, she reflected in the library, her fingers trailing reverently along the spines of the worn leather-bound books lining the mahogany shelves. This had been Mr. Pembroke's sanctuary, a place where he would retreat to ponder the great mysteries of the world. Now, it was hers alone.

Sinking into the plush armchair Pembroke had so often occupied, Charlotte gazed into the dancing flames, allowing their hypnotic rhythm to still the constant whirring of her thoughts. The Pembroke estate, once so foreign and intimidating, had become a comforting presence – a place that, despite its vast size and grandeur, was home. *Had* been her home now for several years.

Charlotte's gaze flickered to the ornate grandfather clock ticking away in the corner, a silent reminder of the relentless march of time. A familiar tightness gripped her chest as she contemplated the weight of her responsibility.

Gathering her courage, Charlotte rose from the armchair, her gaze sweeping the room with newfound purpose. No, Pembroke's legacy depended on her, and she would honor his memory by pushing past her own insecurities and proving herself worthy of the trust he had placed in her. It really was her daily battle.

And a nightly one, too. For she dreamed dreams of failing the man who'd given her a second chance at life. Nightmares, really. Leaving her so soon was too much. At her age, she should be attending socials, gossiping in the park with friends. *Chasing boys.*

But such was not her lot. It never had been.

She was smart. She knew it and felt no arrogance about it. It was true of all the workers and apprentices that came and went in their work for the late Mr. Pembroke. But was it arrogance to think she could understand the depth of something so radical, so new and challenging to the status quo of energy mechanics as they knew it?

How could it be anything but?

You're just a girl.

Yet he'd believed in her.

With a deep breath, she turned and headed towards the workshop, her steps brimming with resolve. Unhealthy obsession or not, she owed him her life.

Always back to work…

Chapter Eight

Months later, a sharp knock at the front-facing workshop door jolted Charlotte from her reverie as she worked. She straightened, smoothing her oil-stained apron as she moved to answer the unexpected visitor. As the door swung open, she found herself face to face with a striking young man, his tailored suit and polished demeanour a stark contrast to the grit and grime of the workshop.

"Miss Pembroke, I presume?" His voice was smooth, tinged with a foreign accent that Charlotte couldn't quite place. "Alexander Blythe, at your service. I represent a group of investors who have taken a keen interest in your work here."

Charlotte regarded him warily, her guard immediately up. "I'm afraid you must be mistaken, Mr. Blythe. Our work here is not for public consumption." Her words were clipped, the wariness in her eyes betraying her mistrust.

But Alexander merely smiled, his eyes sparkling with a genuine appreciation that caught Charlotte off guard. "On the contrary, Miss Pembroke. Your reputation precedes you, and my associates are well aware of the groundbreaking nature of your project. They simply wish to offer their support and resources to see it through to fruition."

Charlotte hesitated, torn between her instinctive caution and the allure of the recognition Alexander's words promised. As she studied him, she couldn't help but notice the keen intelligence in his gaze, the way his eyes flickered over the workshop with an understanding that belied a deeper knowledge of engineering than she had expected.

"I'm a diplomat, of sorts. That is, I uh, bridge connections. Anyhow," he said, smiling warmly once more. *He did have striking eyes.* "Word travels, as it does, and there's an interest in a potential collaboration. Of sorts. As for me personally, I have some experience, and interest, in such matters as well." He glanced around, a bit of genuine excitement and interest in his voice. "I see such advancement here. Particularly in regards to his pet project."

"Well, perhaps we could discuss this further," Charlotte found herself saying, surprising even herself. "Your insights into our work are...intriguing."

Alexander's smile widened, and he inclined his head in agreement. "It would be my pleasure, Miss Pembroke. I have a feeling this could be the beginning of a most fruitful partnership."

As Charlotte led him further into the workshop, a flicker of excitement mingled with the ever-present caution in her heart. Perhaps Alexander Blythe could be the ally she needed to bring her work—no, *Mr. Pembroke's* work, she must remember that—to life.

Despite her initial reservations, she couldn't help but feel a flicker of intrigue. His words had hinted at a genuine appreciation for her work, and his polished demeanour belied a keen intellect that seemed to match her own. There was more to this man she wanted to know.

As they approached the workbench, Charlotte gestured towards the blueprints, her hands darting across from end-to-end. "This is the heart of Project Arcanum—yes, I know, he was quite the eclectic, but it's the device we've been working to bring to life." She paused, her gaze meeting his. "It's a complex undertaking, one that has challenged even the most skilled of engineers. It holds much . . . promise, if you can imagine." She was testing his reaction.

Alexander leaned in, his eyes scanning the diagrams with a look of fascination. "Extraordinary," he murmured, his fingertips ghosting over the plans. "The level of engineering prowess required to design such a device is truly remarkable. And this is possible? Some of these equations are unfamiliar, but I see what he's getting at. Others have tried something like this before him."

Charlotte watched him, a spark of pride igniting within her. "You seem to have a deep understanding of the technical aspects involved. I must admit, I'm surprised to find someone outside of our workshop who can grasp the complexity of the project."

Alexander chuckled, a warmth in his gaze that caught Charlotte off guard. "My dear Miss Pembroke, I've been fascinated by the advancements of engineering and technology since my youth. It's a passion that has only grown stronger with time." He paused, his eyes holding hers. "And I must say, your own dedication to this endeavour is truly inspiring."

Charlotte felt a flush creep up her cheeks at his words, and she quickly averted her gaze, suddenly self-conscious. "It has certainly been a labour of love, Mr. Blythe. Pembroke was a brilliant man, and I feel honoured to be entrusted with carrying on his legacy."

Alexander nodded, his expression sobering. "I can only imagine the weight of that responsibility, especially in a world that is not always kind to the ambitions of women." He placed a hand on her arm, the gesture gentle and understanding. "But I believe you are more than capable of rising to the challenge."

Charlotte blinked, surprised by the sincerity in his words. She had expected skepticism, perhaps even outright dismissal, but instead, she found a kindred spirit – someone who not only grasped the technical complexities of her work but also empathized with the societal obstacles she faced.

"Well," he said, returning his eyes to hers. "What do you think? Unlimited backing and you at the helm of a curious mind alongside yours."

Charlotte's gaze flickered with a mixture of surprise and cautious optimism as she considered Alexander's offer. His words had struck a chord within her, acknowledging the challenges she faced as a woman in a field dominated by men while also recognizing the brilliance of her work.

"Your offer is...most generous, Mr. Blythe," she said carefully, her mind racing with the potential implications. "I must confess, I am intrigued by the prospect of aligning our efforts. Pembroke's project has been a solitary endeavour thus far, and the additional resources and expertise you suggest could prove invaluable." She paused, unsure. "You must have specifics in mind? You are, then, suggesting your talents in particular? As a condition?"

Alexander smiled, his expression warm and reassuring. "I understand your hesitation, Miss Pembroke. This is, after all, a deeply personal endeavour for you. But I can assure you that my associates and I have no desire to undermine your work or Pembroke's legacy. On the contrary, we wish to support and empower *you* to see his vision through."

Charlotte studied him, searching for any hint of deception in his words. Yet, as their eyes met, she found only sincerity and a genuine desire to collaborate. Slowly, she nodded, her resolve strengthening.

"Very well, Mr. Blythe. I am willing to explore this partnership further, on the condition that Pembroke's work remains the sole focus and that I maintain full control over the project's direction and execution."

"Naturally, Miss Pembroke." Alexander inclined his head in agreement. "I would expect nothing less. Your expertise and vision are paramount, and my associates and I are merely here to provide the resources and guidance you require to bring this remarkable endeavour to life."

In the days and weeks that followed, Charlotte found herself deeply immersed in a newfound collaboration with Alexander. Gone were the dismissive attitudes and skeptical glances she had grown accustomed to; instead, she was met with a level of respect and appreciation that she had scarcely dared to hope for.

Alexander proved to be a valuable ally, his connections opening doors to specialized equipment and materials that had previously been out of reach. He listened intently as she explained the technical intricacies of the project, offering insightful suggestions and potential solutions to the challenges she faced.

The camaraderie they developed was unexpected, and Charlotte found herself increasingly drawn to Alexander's sharp mind and unwavering support. *And those gorgeous eyes.* He never once belittled her abilities or questioned her vision, and she marvelled at the way he seemed to grasp the essence of

Pembroke's work with a clarity that rivalled her own.

One particular morning, she found Alexander Blythe striding towards her, a cheerful smile upon his face.

"Good morning, Charlotte," he greeted, his cultured tones sending a flutter through her chest. "I trust you've been making good progress? While I was away the last few day?"

"Mr. Blythe," Charlotte replied, straightening and brushing a stray lock of hair from her face. She never knew when it was appropriate to use his name as he used hers, even though he insisted it was okay. "I have, indeed. The project is progressing, albeit with its fair share of challenges."

Alexander nodded, his gaze sweeping over the various half-finished mechanisms and tools scattered across the worktable. "Your dedication to his legacy is most admirable. And I have no doubt, like your mentor, of your abilities. Actually, it's why I wanted to talk to you."

Charlotte felt a flush creep up her cheeks at his words, and she quickly averted her eyes, suddenly self-conscious. "Thank you. It is a responsibility I take most seriously."

"As you should," Alexander said, his tone reassuring. "Anyway, I believe I may have an opportunity that could further honour your mentor's work."

Charlotte looked up, her curiosity piqued. "An opportunity?"

"Yes," Alexander continued, his eyes sparkling with excitement. "There is growing interest in showcasing innovative technologies at the upcoming Great Exhibition. It's a few years off, but I believe this would be the perfect fit for such a prestigious event. We would need to secure our interest now."

Charlotte's heart raced at the suggestion, a mixture of intrigue and apprehension coursing through her. "The Great Exhibition?" she breathed, her mind whirling with the implications. "That would be an incredible honour, but also a daunting prospect. Surely, the scrutiny and pressure would be immense." It was a *huge* opportunity. A lifetime opportunity.

Alexander nodded and stepped in closer, his expression understanding. "I know it is a significant undertaking, Charlotte. But I have the utmost faith in your abilities, and I believe this could be a once-in-a-lifetime chance to truly immortalize Pembroke's legacy. We can do it. It would need to be draft ready in less than a year. Replicable in two."

Charlotte chewed her lip, her gaze drifting back to the schematics before her. The idea of showcasing Project Arcanum on such a grand stage was both exhilarating and terrifying. It had to work, first. That was a non-starter. But she was getting there.

As if sensing her internal conflict, Alexander reached out and gently placed his hand over hers, the warmth of his touch sending a spark of electricity through her. "I know this is a lot to consider," he said softly. "It's big. But I will be by your side every step of the way, Charlotte. You need not worry."

Charlotte lifted her gaze, her eyes searching his, and in that moment, she felt a connection that went beyond mere friendship. The warmth in his expression, the sincerity in his words – it all resonated deeply within her, and she found herself drawn to this man in a way she had never experienced before.

"Thank you . . . Alexander," she whispered, her fingers curling around his. "I...I appreciate your support more than you know."

He looked down at their hands, then squeezed before looking back up at her, a new look in his eyes that made her heart beat faster.

The following week, Charlotte stood in awe, her gaze sweeping across the sprawling grounds that would soon play host to the grandest exhibition the world had ever seen. Alexander

Blythe stood by her side, a proud smile tugging at the corners of his lips as he observed her reaction.

"Can you see it, Charlotte?" he murmured, his voice laced with excitement. "The sheer scale of this event is truly breathtaking."

Charlotte nodded, her mind racing with the possibilities. Towering structures in gleaming glass and iron rose from the foundations, promising to house the latest innovations from every corner of the globe. The air hummed with the sounds of construction, a symphony of progress that stirred Charlotte's very soul.

"It's... incredible," she breathed, her eyes shining with a mixture of wonder and trepidation. "To think that his work could be displayed among such groundbreaking achievements. The responsibility feels immense."

Alexander placed a reassuring hand on her shoulder, his touch sending a warm flutter through her. "And so it should, my dear. This is your chance to honour Pembroke's legacy and cement your own place in the pantheon of engineering greats. But you are more than capable of rising to the challenge. You have so much to you."

Charlotte turned to face him, her heart swelling with a newfound determination. "You truly believe that, don't you, Alexander?" she murmured, her gaze searching his.

"With every fibre of my being," he replied, his voice soft and sincere. "I have seen the brilliance of your mind, the passion that drives you."

"Then let's do it," she declared, her eyes gleaming with a fierce determination. "Project Arcanum will be seen at the Great Exhibition, a testament to his genius and the boundless potential of engineering. And I will ensure that it succeeds, for his sake and for my own."

Alexander's smile widened, and he gave her shoulder a gentle squeeze. His nearness was intoxicating.

As they turned to continue their exploration of the exhibition grounds, Charlotte felt a stirring of excitement within her. The prospect of showcasing her mentor's lifelong work on such a prestigious stage filled her with a sense of purpose and pride. But more than that, the knowledge that she had a true ally in Alexander – one who believed in her abilities and was willing to help her navigate the challenges ahead – kindled a spark of hope that perhaps, just perhaps, she could forge a future beyond the confines of the workshop. The exhibition was just over two years from now, yet it suddenly loomed large before her.

And she felt up to the challenge. Especially with her new companion by her side. But what kind of companion was he? She knew what she wanted it to be, at least.

That night, as Charlotte pulled her shawl tighter around her shoulders, she hurried down the dimly lit street, the soft glow of a gas lamp flickering overhead. In her hand, she clutched a small paper-wrapped package, the sweet scent of freshly baked biscuits wafting up to greet her.

As she neared the familiar wrought-iron gates of the Hawthornfield Orphanage, Charlotte couldn't help but slow her pace, her gaze drawn to the imposing structure that had once been her home. The memories it stirred - of the cold, spartan rooms and the relentless voice of Mrs. Higgins - filled her with a bittersweet nostalgia.

Charlotte paused, her fingers tracing the intricate metalwork of the gates, as she wondered what the severe matron, Mrs. Higgins, would think of her now. A small smile tugged at the corner of her lips as she imagined the woman's pursed lips and disapproving glare upon seeing her former charge, no longer a timid orphan but a confident, accomplished young woman.

Yet, the temptation to step through those gates and confront her past quickly faded, like a wisp of smoke in the evening breeze. Charlotte shook her head, as if to dispel the lingering shadows of that bygone life, the echoes of Mrs. Higgins' stern voice and the cold, spartan rooms of the orphanage. Instead, she hurried on, her steps quickening as she neared the comforting warmth of home.

Later that night as she slowly brushed out her long, dark hair, her mind drifted to the events of the day, and the growing connection she felt with Alexander.

The man had become a trusted ally, his unwavering support and genuine interest in her work a balm to the constant battles she faced as a woman in the world of engineering. But there was something more, a spark that ignited within her whenever their eyes met or their hands brushed against one another, and she knew it, even if she didn't outwardly acknowledge it.

Or even if he didn't.

Charlotte paused, her fingers stilling in her hair as she contemplated the nature of these newfound feelings. Alexander Blythe was a man of high standing, and she - well, she was just a former orphan, a mere apprentice, albeit maybe one gifted with an exceptional mind by God's grace. Surely, she could not hope for anything more than a professional partnership, no matter how deeply she might wish it. He came from a family of high standing.

Yet, the memory of his warm gaze and the gentle touch of his hand on her arm sent a flutter through her heart, a sensation that both thrilled and unsettled her. Charlotte shook her head, willing the blush from her cheeks as she finished her nightly ritual and climbed into the welcoming embrace of her bed, her mind still awhirl with thoughts of the enigmatic Mr. Blythe.

As she stared up at the ceiling, the flickering shadows dancing across the walls, Charlotte allowed herself a moment of honest reflection. Perhaps, in time, she might find the courage to explore the depths of this connection, to see where it might lead. For now, she would simply cherish the support and companionship Alexander offered, and focus on the task at hand - ensuring that Project Arcanum, and her mentor's legacy, would shine at the Great Exhibition.

Chapter Nine

The year flew by in a whirlwind of progress and setbacks for Charlotte as she poured her heart and soul into Pembroke's now not-so-secret work. While the public knew he was working on something big, they could only speculate as to what. She had made remarkable breakthroughs in her mentor's ambitious endeavor, each triumph fueling her determination to see it through to completion.

She marveled at the potential it had to change the world; a true scientific advancement. Yet, with each milestone achieved, Charlotte couldn't shake the unsettling feeling that unseen forces were conspiring against her. Small, unexplained malfunctions in her equipment, missing critical tools, and even the occasional misplaced blueprint had her on edge, the persistent doubts whispering that someone was deliberately trying to undermine her work.

Frustrated and suspicious, Charlotte decided to confide in the one person she trusted implicitly - Alexander. The young man had become not only a valued collaborator but a cherished confidant, his unwavering support and keen intellect a steadfast anchor in the tumultuous seas of her engineering endeavors.

And she *liked* him. The feelings she had both frightened and excited her, seeing him half the time he was in London.

"So. I fear that someone is deliberately sabotaging my progress," Charlotte admitted, her brow furrowed with a mixture of concern and determination. "The incidents have become too frequent to be mere coincidence." She paused, her fingers drumming anxiously against the worn wooden table as she searched Alexander's face for any sign of disbelief or dismissal. His unwavering gaze, however, conveyed only a quiet understanding.

Alexander's brow creased with a contemplative frown as he listened intently, his sharp gaze reflecting the wheels turning in his mind. "That is a grave concern, indeed," he murmured, his voice measured and thoughtful. "Have you any inkling as to who might be behind these acts?"

Charlotte shook her head, her fingers fidgeting with the worn edge of her dress. *I need to take time for myself one of these days.* "I can only speculate, but the thought that someone would go to such lengths to undermine my work is... unsettling." She paused, her gaze meeting Alexander's. "I feel as if I'm being watched, as if there are shadows lurking in the corners, ready to snatch away all that I've worked for. Am I going crazy? Oh, I know how it sound, *ugh*."

Reaching across the table, Alexander placed his hand over Charlotte's, his touch warm and reassuring. "No. There are many who would prefer not to share the glory at the Exhibition. Whoever is responsible, we shall not allow them to succeed," he declared, his voice firm and resolute. "Here now. I shall support you fully in uncovering the truth and ending this sabotage, Charlotte. You have my word. I wouldn't be here if I didn't intend to see it through. My time here is for this very purpose, okay? We got this."

Charlotte nodded, her fingers tightening around Alexander's hand as a glimmer of relief washed over her. "I am grateful for your support, Alexander. This task has felt increasingly...lonely, of late." She looked down at their hands, smiling a little. "Honestly, now that you're back again, I feel as though I can face anything." Charlotte was grateful for his presence, knowing she would need his help in the coming days. She squeezed his hand, taking courage from his presence.

Just then, a sharp rap at the workshop door interrupted the tender moment. Charlotte's head snapped up, her expression schooled into one of polite neutrality as she rose to greet the visitor.

She faltered, her eyes widening slightly as she took in the familiar face. "Mr. Hawkins. Forgive me, I was not expecting you." Geoffrey Hawkins, the persistent journalist, had been pursuing her for an interview. She had been wary of his prying questions in the past, knowing he was determined to uncover the details of Pembroke's project and her own role in it. But he hadn't reached out in a month, and never before at her home.

The journalist stood on the threshold, a friendly smile crinkling the corners of his eyes. "Miss Pembroke," he greeted warmly, doffing his hat. "I do hope I'm not interrupting anything important."

Charlotte glanced back at Alexander, who had also risen to his feet, before turning her attention back to the journalist. "Not at all, Mr. Hawkins. Please, do come in." She ushered him inside. He was certainly persistent, which she admired in a way.

"To what do I owe the pleasure of your visit?" she inquired, gesturing for him to take a seat. "I must confess, I was not aware you would be calling."

Geoffrey settled into the chair, his gaze sweeping the workshop with undisguised interest. "Ah, yes, well, I'm afraid this is a rather...impromptu visit." He cleared his throat, his expression turning more serious. "You see, I've been tasked with writing another piece on the legacy of Mr. Pembroke, and I was hoping to have some of your time. To uncover the latest happenings."

Charlotte felt her stomach tighten with unease at Geoffrey's words. Another article about Mr. Pembroke's legacy? The very thought made her uneasy. Too many prying eyes had already cast their judgement upon her and her mentor's work. She knew some circles in London had spoken of their relationship and the fact that she was now the owner of his estate. Good press, bad press . . . she didn't care for any of it.

"I see," she said cautiously, glancing once more towards Alexander. The young man's expression had grown more reserved, his keen gaze flickering between the journalist and Charlotte. "And what, precisely, are you hoping to uncover, Mr. Hawkins?"

Geoffrey leaned forward, his elbows resting on his knees as he fixed Charlotte with an earnest look. "I'll be frank, Miss Pembroke. There has been a great deal of speculation and...rumor, surrounding the work you and Mr. Pembroke were undertaking. As a journalist, it's my duty to separate fact from fiction. From my understanding, this could go one of several ways. Something this big... Well, believability and all that..."

Charlotte's jaw tightened slightly, her fingers curling against the fabric of her skirt. "I see," she repeated, her tone measured. "And what, pray tell, have you heard?"

The journalist held up a placating hand. "Now, now, I mean no offense. I simply wish to understand the truth of the matter - for the sake of Mr. Pembroke's legacy, as well as your own." He paused, his gaze flickering towards Alexander once more. "And perhaps, to shed light on this 'Project Arcanum' that has become the talk of the engineering and scientific communities."

Charlotte felt a surge of protectiveness wash over her. Project Arcanum was hers and Mr. Pembroke's to share, not the idle gossip of the masses. "I'm afraid I don't feel comfortable discussing the details of my mentor's work," she said firmly. "Mr. Pembroke valued his privacy, and I intend to honor that."

Geoffrey nodded slowly, his expression thoughtful. "I understand your hesitation, Miss Pembroke. But surely you can appreciate the public's curiosity. After all, the work you and Mr. Pembroke were undertaking could very well change the course of history." He leaned back in his chair, his gaze steady, waving his hand. "Or so some say. I simply wish to ensure that his legacy is recorded accurately."

Charlotte opened her mouth to respond, but Alexander spoke up before she could, his voice low and measured. "Mr. Hawkins, I'm certain you can appreciate the sensitive nature of Miss Pembroke's work. As her mentor's protégée, she is understandably cautious about revealing too much, lest it jeopardize the success of her endeavors." He paused, offering the journalist a polite smile. "Perhaps we could discuss a more...general overview of Mr. Pembroke's life and contributions to the field of engineering. I'm sure Miss Pembroke would be amenable to that."

Charlotte shot Alexander a grateful look, relieved to have his support in deflecting the journalist's prying questions. She turned her attention back to Geoffrey, her expression calmer, yet still resolute. "Mr. Hawkins, I hope you can understand that my focus must remain on honoring Mr. Pembroke's legacy through my own work. I'm afraid I cannot provide you with the specific details you seek."

Charlotte's gaze remained steady as she met Geoffrey's probing stare. The journalist's brow furrowed slightly, and she could see the wheels turning in his mind, no doubt considering how to best coax the details he sought from her.

"I see," he said slowly, his gaze shifting between the two of them. "Then perhaps you might be willing to grant me a full interview of a different nature, Miss Pembroke? I'm certain our readers would be interested to learn more about your own journey as Mr. Pembroke's protégée. With a look at the trials you must be facing. In your particular position. Can I be frank for a moment? I see opportunity for us both here. Yes, I stand to gain from a scoop such as this. But think of the good it can do for you as well! To be taken seriously."

Charlotte hesitated, her mind racing. An interview would undoubtedly bring more unwanted attention, but she couldn't help but wonder if it might also be an opportunity to shape the narrative, to control the story of her mentor's legacy.

Alexander must have sensed her internal conflict, for he spoke up once more, his voice low and soothing. "Mr. Hawkins, I believe Miss Pembroke would be more comfortable sharing her story at a later date, once she has had time to properly reflect on her experiences." He paused, offering the journalist a polite smile. "Perhaps we could arrange something once her work on her current project is done?"

Geoffrey's expression shifted, a glimmer of understanding dawning in his eyes. "Ah, I see. Well, in that case, I shall be sure to follow up with you both in the future." He rose from his chair, dipping his head in a respectful nod. "Thank you for your time, Miss Pembroke, Mr. Blythe. I look forward to it."

Charlotte released a breath she hadn't realized she'd been holding, her shoulders sagging slightly as the journalist took his leave. She turned to Alexander, a faint smile tugging at the corners of her lips. "Thank you, for your help, Alexander.""

Alexander returned her smile, his gaze warm and reassuring. "Of course, Charlotte. I could see it in your eyes, and I knew you needed an ally in that moment." He reached out, gently squeezing her hand, once again giving her heart pause at the touch.

Over the next few weeks, Charlotte felt herself growing increasingly paranoid as more and more "accidents"—if that's what they were—continued to happen in the workshop. At first, it had been minor things - tools that had been misplaced, or a part that had been faulty, causing the prototype to fail. But the problems only seemed to increase, and now Charlotte found herself second-guessing everyone, even those she had come to trust.

People came and went, but she knew it couldn't be any of the workers, they may not have loved her like Mr. Pembroke, but they loved and respected him too much. Yet still, with his tradition of his workshop continuing to be the epicenter of both his private business and place of apprenticeship, many hands touched her world daily.

Yet it felt like for every step forward, she took two steps back.

Frowning as she read over her notes, as well as those of her adopted father, Charlotte had the distinct impression that someone was watching her, waiting to pounce as soon as she made any progress. She looked around, but saw no one. Still, she had a lot of work ahead of her, and the threat of failure loomed large in her mind, no matter how skilled she had become.

It was during one such moment of self-doubt that Thomas Keating, Pembroke's longtime apprentice, unexpectedly returned to the workshop. She wanted to lay her troubles at his feet, but he was rarely there himself, and that wasn't fair anyway. He just wore his emotions on his sleeve.

Charlotte looked up, her eyes narrowing as the familiar figure walked through the door. She'd been so engrossed in her numbers and notes that she hadn't noticed him enter. She had heard that Keating had left Pembroke's employ years ago to pursue his own engineering endeavors elsewhere. Yet here he was, standing before her, a small smile on his lips. Charlotte's heart skipped a beat as a wave of mixed emotions washed over her. Part of her was glad to see a familiar face, but the other part of her couldn't help but wonder what he was doing here. She straightened up, her face neutral as she waited for him to speak, the unease she had been feeling moments before now heightened by his sudden reappearance.

"Thomas," she greeted him warily, setting down the schematic she had been meticulously studying. "How are you? This is an unexpected visit."

Keating offered her a thin smile, his gaze sweeping the workshop. "Miss Pembroke. I must admit, I was quite shocked to hear of Pembroke's passing and your subsequent inheritance of his estate."

Charlotte's fingers tightened around the edge of the workbench, her mind racing. "Yes, well, it was Mr. Pembroke's wish that I continue his work." Her eyes narrowed slightly. "So . . . how can I help you?"

Keating merely smiled. "Charlotte, I'm afraid I've returned to see to the completion of

Pembroke's *true* legacy." He stepped closer, his gaze boring into hers. "After all, who better to oversee such a momentous project than his most trusted apprentice?"

Charlotte felt her stomach twist with unease at the implication in Keating's words. "I'm afraid I don't understand. This workshop and all of Pembroke's work now belong to me."

"Ah, yes. Well, I apologize, I'm afraid that's where you may be slightly mistaken. Pembroke may have favored you, but I was the one he truly confided in. I know the secrets of Project Arcanum, the true scope of its potential. I'm here to talk to you about it."

Sudden movement at the workshop door drew Charlotte's attention, and she felt a surge of relief at the sight of Alexander striding towards them, his expression grave.

"Miss Pembroke," he said, his voice low and urgent. "I'm afraid I have some troubling news." His gaze flicked towards Keating, a hint of suspicion flashing in his eyes. "It appears someone has tampered with the primary power source for your latest prototype." He turned to Charlotte, his brow creased with concern, rubbing his hands through his hair. "I fear it may be beyond repair. We're uh . . . set back months at this point." He said the last a little more for her ears only.

Charlotte's heart sank, her eyes darting between the two men.

"I see," she said slowly, her mind racing. Turning to Keating, Charlotte squared her shoulders, her voice unwavering. "Please excuse me. Let's set a time to talk later this week perhaps. It was good to see you again."

Keating bowed his head briefly and politely excused himself.

She was in over her head. Had been for some time, really. Her passion was both her blessing, and now her curse, it seemed.

The scents outside and the vibrant colours in a city full of bustling industry and sounds that filled the air at all times gave her time to collect herself. Charlotte's shoulders sagged with a heavy sigh as she led Geoffrey Hawkins through the verdant park near the Pembroke estate. The journalist had been insistent on speaking with her, and after much deliberation, she had agreed to grant him an off-the-record interview.

As they strolled along the winding path, the late afternoon sunlight dappling the ground, Charlotte couldn't shake the feeling that he knew more than he was letting on.

"I must admit, Miss Pembroke, I've been hearing some rather...intriguing rumors about your work and the setbacks you've had," Hawkins began, his tone conversational.

Charlotte glanced sidelong at him, her expression carefully neutral. "I'm afraid I don't know what you mean, Mr. Hawkins."

The journalist chuckled lightly. "Come now, my dear. I may be a mere scribe, but I have my ear to the ground. There are whispers of fierce competition surrounding your project." Hawkins turned to face her, his gaze keen. "I'm simply saying that there may be...other parties with a vested interest in seeing your endeavors come to a standstill." He paused, his expression darkening. "And I fear they may not be playing by the rules."

What use was it hiding anymore? "So. I'm not imagining it, and it's not an accident."

Hawkins nodded solemnly. "I'm afraid so. And while I may not know the specifics, I felt it was my duty to warn you." He reached out, giving her arm a gentle squeeze. "You must be vigilant, Charlotte. There are those who would do anything to get their hands on Pembroke's legacy. And to upstage you in the Exhibition. You know," he continued after a moment's thought, "I cared about Mr. Pembroke a lot. We become close after a while. I think he'd want you to be careful moving forward. I'm being sincere, no agenda here. I can learn things others can't, by the very nature of my position, and who I've worked with before."

Charlotte's mind raced as she processed Hawkins' words. She had suspected that the strange incidents in the workshop were no mere coincidence, but to hear it confirmed sent a chill down her spine. Pembroke's legacy was hers to uphold, and she would be damned if she let anyone take that from her.

"Thank you, Mr. Hawkins," she said quietly, her jaw set with determination. "I appreciate you taking the time to share this information with me. You can be assured that I will be on my guard and look at who I'm working with, inside and outside of the workshop. I'll be careful."

Hawkins offered her a small, knowing smile. "I have no doubt of that, my dear. And please, should you ever need a sympathetic ear - or perhaps a bit of off-the-record assistance - you need only ask." *Maybe he is an ally after all,* she thought.

As they continued their stroll, Charlotte's mind whirled with the implications of Hawkins' warning. She would need to be more vigilant than ever.

And more careful of who you trust.

Chapter Ten

Charlotte's fingers trembled as she held the worn, yellowed letters in her hands. The delicate paper crinkled under her touch, the words fading but still legible. She had stumbled upon these hidden missives by chance, tucked away in a trunk that Henrietta had recently recovered from one of Mr. Pembroke's old offices. The housekeeper had brought them to Charlotte, a somber expression on her face. "I think you should read these, my dear," she had said, her voice soft.

As Charlotte pored over the letters, her heart raced. *All this time, he knew who I was. He knew about my family.* Her birth father and Mr. Pembroke had been friends. Henriette was just as surprised to learn of it, but it made little difference now that both were gone.

He'd taken her in because he *did* care. It made his loss even more sad, now. Yet there so much more to know!

Clutching the letters tightly, Charlotte knew she had to seek answers. There was only one person she could turn to - Lord Edwin Mercer, a respected patron of engineering who had been acquainted with Pembroke during her late mentor's younger years.

"Surely, he'll see me?" she asked Henrietta the next day.

Henrietta watched Charlotte with a concerned expression. "Are you certain you wish to seek an audience with Lord Mercer? It could dredge up painful memories."

Charlotte paused, considering her housekeeper's words. "I must know the truth, Henrietta. Mr. Pembroke kept so much from me, and now that he's gone..." Her voice trailed off, the weight of her mentor's absence palpable.

Henrietta reached out and squeezed Charlotte's hand. "Then I shall make the arrangements. Lord Mercer has always held you in high regard; I'm sure he will grant you an audience."

Two days later, Charlotte found herself ushered into Lord Mercer's grand study, the imposing man rising from his chair to greet her.

"Miss Pembroke," he said, his voice warm. "What a pleasant surprise. To what do I owe this visit?"

Charlotte took a steadying breath. "Lord Mercer, I... I've come into possession of some letters. Letters that suggest my birth father was acquainted with Mr. Pembroke." She paused, searching his face for any flicker of recognition.

Lord Mercer's brow furrowed, and he gestured for Charlotte to take a seat. "I see. Please, tell me what you know."

As Charlotte recounted the contents of the letters, Lord Mercer listened intently, his expression growing graver with each passing moment. When she finished, he clasped his hands, his gaze fixed on the ornate rug beneath their feet.

"Your birth father was a dear friend of Richard's," he began, his tone somber. "They worked together closely, until..." He hesitated, his eyes flickering with a mix of sorrow and regret.

Charlotte leaned forward, her heart pounding. "Until what, my lord?"

Lord Mercer met her gaze, his eyes filled with a profound sadness. "Until the accident that took your father's life. Richard... he blamed himself, you see. I'm sure that is why he took you in, to honor your father's memory."

"Why didn't I know any of this?"

"Ah, yes, that is where the story becomes more complicated." Mercer paused, his fingers drumming thoughtfully on the desk. "Your parents were killed in a terrible accident, one that Pembroke was also involved in. He lived, your parents did not. Your father was considered a genius, you know. They were so close, and it was a devastating blow to him, and in the aftermath, he vowed to find you one day and maybe try to connect. You were just a young thing, you wouldn't remember him. He felt so guilty about what happened to them. He hoped you would have found another family, I think. Some of this, you understand, is speculation, although I have followed your progress, my dear."

The revelation struck Charlotte like a physical blow, and she struggled to process the implications. Pembroke had known her all along, had taken her in and mentored her, all the while carrying the weight of her parents' tragic demise.

"But why?" she breathed, her voice barely above a whisper. "Why did he never tell me?"

Mercer's expression softened with empathy. "I suspect he wanted to spare you the pain of knowing the truth. Pembroke cared for you deeply, Charlotte, and he wished to provide you with a stable future, even if it meant keeping his connection to your family a secret. I suspect he would have seen it as selfish, and the more he waited, well . . . anyway. We're all human. But I'm sure he loved you very much."

Charlotte felt her eyes sting with tears, a tangle of emotions overwhelming her. Pembroke's steadfast guidance, his unwavering belief in her abilities – it all made sense now, tinged with a bittersweet understanding.

"What else can you tell me?" she asked, her voice quivering. "About my parents, about their work, about–"

Mercer raised a hand, silencing her gently. "I will share what I know, my dear, but we should eat, I'm afraid my stomach will interrupt too much with its growls and protests. Please, stay for supper? Let's talk over a nice meal."

Charlotte stepped through the door of the Pembroke estate late in the evening, the weight of the day's revelations heavy on her shoulders. The grand hall was dimly lit, but the warm glow of lanterns cast a welcoming ambiance, softening the shadows that seemed to cling to the corners. She couldn't help but feel a sense of unease, as if the very walls of this familiar home had become tinged with a newfound uncertainty, the once comforting atmosphere now tinged with an unsettling edge.

"Ah, there you are, my dear!" Henrietta's familiar voice, laced with its usual maternal warmth, called out from the kitchen, snapping Charlotte from her troubled thoughts. The housekeeper's round, matronly figure appeared in the doorway, her spectacles perched precariously on the end of her nose. "I was just about to send one of the footmen to fetch you. I assume you've eaten, then?"

Smoothing a hand over her brow, Charlotte made her way towards the kitchen. "I dined, but oddly I'm still hungry, it smells delicious. Perhaps a small plate."

"You were out awfully late, Charlotte. I was starting to worry," the housekeeper chided, but her tone was laced with the affection of a mother figure. Charlotte felt a pang of guilt for causing Henrietta concern.

"I'm so sorry, Henrietta. My meeting with Lord Mercer ran longer than expected," Charlotte replied, offering an apologetic smile. "But it was good." She knew Henrietta cared deeply for her, and the older woman's worry was a testament to the bond they had forged over the years.

Henrietta waved a dismissive hand. "No matter, no matter. The cook and I quite enjoyed the meal together. Kept me company, of course. Cozy stolen moments, you see. I may be getting bigger, but he can still fit his hands around me."

She winked conspiratorially, and Charlotte couldn't help but smile at the implication. It was a small moment of levity in the midst of her turmoil. "Maybe one day he'll make it official. Wouldn't be the worst thing he could do if he's going to steal kisses that often."

"Well, I'm glad you didn't wait on me," said Charlotte, accepting the steaming plate Henrietta handed her. The familiar comfort of the kitchen and Henrietta's motherly presence were a welcome respite. "And for the record, I give you both a thumb's up. Lord knows you two kiss loud enough to wake all of London, with all that lip smacking."

Henrietta's cheeks flushed a bright pink at the teasing. "Oh, you hush now, you cheeky girl," the housekeeper scolded, the corners of her mouth twitching upwards.

Settling onto one of the worn kitchen stools, Charlotte savored the hearty stew, the familiar flavors providing a soothing balm for her troubled mind. As she ate, she watched Henrietta bustle about the kitchen, humming a soft tune under her breath.

"You know, I wouldn't be surprised if the cook proposed sooner rather than later," Charlotte mused, unable to resist another playful jab. "He's been eyeing you like a hungry wolf, that one."

Henrietta paused, her hands stilling as she turned to face Charlotte, a wistful expression on her face. "Ah, my dear, you jest, but sometimes I wonder if it's not too late for me. The years have a way of slipping by, don't they?" She sighed, her gaze growing distant.

Charlotte's brow furrowed as she watched the change in Henrietta's demeanor. Setting down her spoon, she reached across the table and squeezed the housekeeper's wrinkled hand. "Henrietta, don't talk like that. You have so much life in you yet. And the cook adores you, anyone can see that."

The older woman smiled, her eyes crinkling at the corners. "You're a good girl, Charlotte. Always looking out for this old heart of mine." She patted Charlotte's hand affectionately. "But enough of my ramblings. Tell me, how did your meeting with Lord Mercer go? I can see it weighs heavily on you."

Charlotte's expression sobered, and she withdrew her hand, her fingers tracing the worn wooden grain of the table. "It was... enlightening, to say the least." She recounted the revelations about her birth parents, Pembroke's connection to their tragic demise, and the guilt that had driven him to take her in.

As Charlotte spoke, Henrietta's face grew grave, her eyes filling with a deep sadness. "Oh, my dear child," she murmured, reaching out to brush a stray lock of hair from Charlotte's face. "I had no idea. Poor Richard, carrying that burden all these years."

Charlotte nodded, her gaze downcast. "I don't know how to feel, Henrietta. Part of me is grateful that Pembroke cared for me, but the other part wishes he had been honest from the start." She paused, her fingers curling into a fist. "And now he's gone, and I'm left with so many unanswered questions."

Henrietta's expression softened with empathy, and she moved around the table to pull Charlotte into a warm embrace. "Shh, my dear, I know. It's a lot to take in. But you're not alone, you hear? I'm here, and I'll do whatever I can to help you find the answers you seek."

Charlotte leaned into the comforting hug, feeling the weight of her grief and confusion begin to lift, if only for a moment. In Henrietta's arms, she found the solace she so desperately needed, even as the shadows of the past continued to linger.

Bidding Henrietta a good night, Charlotte made her way to her room, the weight of the day's events dragging at her steps. She sank down onto the edge of her bed, exhausted.

At her age, she was starting to think of her own family someday.

But first you have to find the one love, she thought as she drifted off.

Chapter Eleven

The morning sun streamed through the lace curtains of Charlotte's bedchamber, casting a warm glow that woke her gently from her sleep. A soft breeze carried the scent of freshly trimmed roses from the gardens, a fleeting but needed reminder of all the beauty that existed beyond the workshop walls where she spent most of her life these days.

Charlotte's fingers traced the intricate etchings on a brass cog by her bedside, her mind already consumed by the day's tasks. It was not as pretty as nature, but the machinery beside her was just as intoxicating in many ways. With a steadying breath, she made her way downstairs, her footsteps echoing through the quiet corridors.

Alexander was already waiting in the main workshop, his sleeves rolled up as he pored over a stack of blueprints. He glanced up at her approach, a warm smile spreading across his features. "Ah,

Charlotte. What do you say, are you ready to bring this marvel to life? Almost there."

She nodded, settling herself and arranging her tools with practiced precision. The weight of the moment was not lost on her – the successful completion of this part of the project would be a triumph, but failure could tarnish her reputation beyond repair. She knew now what it was meant to do. But the tolerances for error were next to none. It was precise, and there was no other way.

With deft movements, she began meticulously aligning what she needed, her brow furrowed in concentration. Alexander watched in rapt silence, his presence both reassuring and unnerving. She could feel the weight of his gaze, a subtle reminder of the bond they had forged over countless late nights spent huddled over schematics.

As the last component slid into place for one of the final pieces, Charlotte let out a shuddering breath, her fingers trembling ever so slightly. She stepped back, her eyes drinking in the sight of the near-completed project, a testament to years of toil and sacrifice.

Alexander moved to stand beside her, his shoulder brushing against hers in a fleeting moment of contact that sent a frisson of electricity through her veins. Their eyes met, and she saw the depths of his admiration mirrored in his gaze, a silent acknowledgment of the connection that had blossomed between them, one that dared to cross the boundaries of professionalism.

"Do an inspection?" She nodded to the plans, and the two of them proceeded to check arc levels, tensions and everything needed meticulously against the plans on the table. He'd been almost right on everything, Mr. Pembroke. But some changes had had to be made. Still, she marveled at his genius; he couldn't have foreseen some of the problems inherent in something groundbreaking like this, yet he'd been right about most of his theory.

She bent down to make notes, the rhythmic scratching of Charlotte's pencil against parchment stilled as the drawing room door swung open with a forceful thud. Thomas Keating strode in, his gaze sweeping over the array of blueprints strewn across the table.

"Well, well, if it isn't the lady engineer and her foreign accomplice," he said. "Hard at work, I see."

Charlotte stiffened, her fingers tightening around her pencil as Alexander rose to his feet beside her. "Mr. Keating," she greeted, her tone clipped. "*Thomas* . . . What can I help you with now?"

Keating's lip curled as he snatched up one of the blueprints, his eyes roving over the intricate schematics. She let him. "Merely inspecting the work you claim as your own," he remarked, his voice hinting subtly at contempt. "Tell me, how much of this grand design truly stems from your own mind, and how much is simply the regurgitated genius of the late Mr. Pembroke? I wouldn't know because you never let me in. I assume for obvious reasons."

Charlotte felt her cheeks flush, but before she could respond, Alexander stepped forward, his bearing radiating a quiet authority. "Miss Pembroke's contributions are her own," he stated firmly. "I would caution against making baseless accusations. There's good reason he favoured her, even when you were here."

But Keating was not so easily dissuaded. "Is that so?" He rounded on Charlotte, his eyes glinting with malice. "Then perhaps you would care to explain the inner workings of this sophisticated mechanism without the aid of your mentor's precious notes? Can you even? How much is just show?"

Fine. I'll play your stupid game, Thomas. Charlotte drew a steadying breath, willing her thundering heart to still as she met Keating's contemptuous stare head-on. She would not allow him to cow her, not after all she had endured to reach this point. With a deft hand, she rearranged the scattered blueprints, barely containing the emotions in her face.

"This central mechanism," she began, her voice ringing with quiet authority, "functions on a principle of electrodynamic induction. The copper coils here generate a rotating magnetic field, which in turn drives the armature and..."

Word by meticulous word, Charlotte laid bare the intricacies of her design, her explanations flowing with the practiced ease of one who had committed every nuance to memory. As she spoke, Keating's sneer faltered, his eyes betraying a reluctant glimmer of begrudging respect.

At last, Charlotte fell silent, her chin tilted ever so slightly as she awaited Keating's response. For a tense moment, he said nothing, his gaze flickering between her and the blueprints. Finally, he gave a curt nod, seeming to deflate as the fight drained from him.

"Well...it would appear your grasp of the principles is sound," he muttered, his tone laced with the barest hint of approval. With a final contemptuous sniff, he turned on his heel and stalked from the room, leaving a charged silence in his wake.

Charlotte exhaled slowly, her shoulders sagging as the adrenaline ebbed from her veins. Beside her, Alexander's hand found the small of her back in a subtle, steadying gesture.

"You handled that admirably," he murmured, his words a warm balm against the sting of Keating's challenge.

"Ha. Maybe. Yet I sometimes wonder if I should have revoked the open door policy he left in place," she murmured. Yet, even as she basked in Alexander's reassurance, a tendril of unease coiled within her. Keating's jealousy and resentment were far from extinguished, and she knew all too well the damage such petty machinations could wreak.

Later, as they walked the sprawling grounds of the estate, Charlotte found herself confiding her fears to Alexander. "Keating's influence should not be underestimated," she admitted, her brow furrowed. "You know, a single whispered doubt in the right ear could undo all we've worked for. It shouldn't be about politics, and yet—"

"And yet it always is," he finished. "You're not the only game in town with a solution of this kind. It's the new rage in theory and academia. Nor the only one with so much at stake, including fame, notoriety and money."

"Why can't it just be simple? Who can anyone trust, really."

Alexander's expression grew pensive as he considered her words. "You're right to be cautious," he conceded. "But you mustn't allow Keating's envy to diminish your accomplishments." His fingers brushed against hers, a fleeting touch that sent a frisson of electricity through her veins. "You have achieved something remarkable, Charlotte. I, for one, have no doubts. You're . . . an extraordinary woman." He turned to her then, their faces close as they stopped to look at each other. "In many ways. I . . . I know that's forward, but you are."

Charlotte looked down to hide the color rising in her cheeks.

"I feel the same way. Not about you being a remarkable woman, ugh, I - you know what I mean!" They laughed then, and the tension seemed to dissipate.

But a tension of another kind had taken deeper root. She had fallen for Alexander.

The rhythmic clang of tools against metal rang out in the workshop, punctuated by the occasional hiss of steam from the nearby boiler. Charlotte and Alexander worked in companionable silence, their movements synchronised in a well-practised dance of industry. They both wore their goggles at this stage, fearful of accidents and the power in front of them, lest it should escape unbidden. Stranger things had happened.

A sharp rap at the door shattered her concentration. Charlotte and Alexander exchanged a guarded look, the ghost of Keating's sneering visage flitting across their minds. Surely he wouldn't return so soon after the schooling she'd given him?

The door creaked open to reveal not the contemptuous engineer but rather the slightly rumpled figure of Geoffrey Hawkins, the journalist who had been covering Charlotte's efforts.

"Miss Pembroke, Mr. Blythe," he greeted with a polite nod, his eyes roving over the nearly assembled apparatus with undisguised curiosity. "I hope I'm not interrupting?"

Charlotte drew herself up, angling her body to shield the delicate workings from Hawkins' prying gaze. *Only because my adopted father wanted it,* she reminded herself, trying not to be annoyed at the seeming constant comings and goings of others. *Although the rule had been meant to encourage innovation, not stifle it.* "Not at all, Mr. Hawkins. How may we assist you?"

The journalist withdrew a sheaf of papers from his satchel, his expression grave. "I'm afraid I come bearing ill tidings. It would seem our esteemed Mr. Keating—was he here earlier, by the way?—has been engaging in rather unsavoury tactics in an effort to discredit your work."

With a deft hand, he spread the documents across the worktable, revealing a series of scathing letters and articles, each one dripping with vitriol and casting aspersions on Charlotte's character and capabilities.

Alexander's jaw tightened as he scanned the damning evidence, his fingers clenching into white-knuckled fists. "This is outrageous. I know he's jealous, that he feels maligned… but to think he would stoop to such underhanded means…"

Charlotte's mind reeled, a sickening sense of betrayal churning in her gut. "The nerve of that wretched man," she murmured, her voice trembling with barely contained fury. "After all I've accomplished, all I've endured…"

Hawkins nodded, his expression one of grim understanding. "Make no mistake, his efforts extend far beyond mere words. I have reason to believe he has been actively attempting to sway loyalties within these very walls, to turn your own staff against you."

"They're not my staff," she murmured for what seemed the hundredth time in the last year. But her mind was elsewhere to care too much as she considered. Was he responsible for the setbacks? Did he have someone on the inside. It was disheartening to consider.

Not unlikely, truthfully, she thought. She drew in a deep breath, calming herself. She wanted to believe the best in others. Whatever role he played, even he couldn't be so brash as to sabotage her work out of spite.

A heavy silence descended over the workshop as the weight of Hawkins' revelation sank in. *Something* was up. Charlotte felt the world shift beneath her feet, the foundations upon which she had built her life's work suddenly rendered unstable.

Sensing her distress, Alexander laid a reassuring hand upon her arm. "We cannot allow him to undermine your achievements, Charlotte," he murmured, his voice low and intense. "Not after everything you've sacrificed."

Hawkins cleared his throat, his eyes bright with the spark of opportunity. "Perhaps, then, it is time to take a more proactive stance," he suggested. "An alliance of sorts, if you will. I can lend my pen to the task of exposing Keating's duplicity and ensuring your rightful place in the annals of innovation is secured."

Charlotte regarded him for a long moment, her mind whirring with the implications of his proposition. To openly align herself with the press was a bold move, one that could either cement her legacy or leave her reputation in tatters.

Yet, as she met Alexander's steadfast gaze, she knew there was no other viable course of action. With a resolute nod, she extended her hand to Hawkins. "Very well, Mr. Hawkins. Let us forge this alliance and bring the truth to light."

"Good! Now, I have a wonderful idea."

Charlotte surveyed the assembled guests with a critical eye, her fingers drumming an anxious rhythm against the worktable. Hawkins had pulled out all the stops, ensuring that only the most influential members of London's scientific and academic elite had received invitations to this private demonstration of Project Arcanum.

It was a large room, though it still felt crowded. Each face in the crowd represented a potential ally or foe, their presence serving as both an invaluable opportunity and a profound risk. One misstep, one errant slip of the tongue, and the delicate balance of power could come crashing down around her.

Alexander caught her eye from across the room, offering her a subtle nod of reassurance. His unwavering belief in her abilities had been an anchor amidst the choppy waters of doubt and sabotage. With a steadying breath, Charlotte straightened her shoulders and strode to the center of the workshop, her bearing radiating a quiet confidence.

"Distinguished guests," she began, her clear voice cutting through the murmured conversations. "I thank you all for attending this exclusive demonstration. What you are about to witness is the culmination of years of tireless effort, a feat of engineering that will propel us into a new era of innovation." She then instructed those nearest to don goggles, just in case.

As she spoke, Charlotte's gaze flickered to the doorway, where the squat, unpleasant figure of Thomas Keating lingered. His lips were twisted into a contemptuous sneer, but there was an unmistakable glint of unease in his eyes – a testament to the efficacy of their plan. His invitation was no accident.

With a subtle flick of her wrist, Charlotte set the apparatus in motion, the intricate mechanisms whirring to life with a symphony of hisses and clanks. The crowd leaned forward, enraptured, as she deftly explained the principles behind each component, her words flowing with the practiced ease of a master orator.

From the corner of her eye, she noted Hawkins scribbling furiously in his notebook, no doubt capturing every nuance of her presentation for his impending exposé. Beside him, Alexander watched with rapt attention, his expression one of undisguised pride.

As the demonstration reached its crescendo, Charlotte could practically taste the awe that rippled through the assembled guests. Murmurs of impressed exclamation mingled with the rhythmic chugging of the machinery, a resounding validation of her efforts.

At last, the apparatus ground to a halt, and Charlotte stepped back, her chest rising and falling with exhilaration. For a fleeting moment, the room was utterly silent, until a smattering of polite applause erupted, quickly swelling into a thunderous ovation.

"And this is ready?"

"This is using a new procedure?"

"What's the output on a larger scale?" asked yet another.

As the guests descended upon Charlotte with a flurry of congratulations and more probing questions, Alexander slipped to her side, his hand finding the small of her back in a subtle, steadying gesture.

"Well done, my dear," he murmured, his voice rich with undisguised admiration. "Your triumph is unassailable."

Charlotte allowed herself a small, victorious smile, basking in the warmth of Alexander's approval.

Finally, as the last of the guests filed out, offering final words of congratulations and praise, Charlotte felt a profound sense of relief wash over her. The demonstration had been an unqualified success, a resounding validation of the countless hours she had poured into bringing Project Arcanum to fruition. At this point, verifications would have to be made, peer-reviews given access. But if they believed her claims, it meant a shift had occurred in the industry. Worldwide, potentially. Truly, the potential was as yet unknown.

Turning to look at Alexander, she saw he was already looking at her, with an expression that mirrored her own joy and relief. At that moment, it felt like some invisible wall had fallen away, leaving only the undeniable bond that had grown between them, strengthened by the trials they had been through together.

Without a word, Alexander closed the distance between them, his hand coming to rest at the curve of her waist in a gesture that was at once familiar and electrifying. Charlotte's breath caught in her throat as she met his piercing gaze, the weight of unspoken truths and shared burdens passing between them in a wordless exchange.

They both knew what they wanted.

Their lips met in a heated kiss, shattering the fragile constraints of propriety. Charlotte felt a surge of triumph and possibility course through her as Alexander's strong arms encircled her waist, pulling her close. In that moment, all the yearning they had both held at bay for so long was unleashed, their bodies and souls intertwining as if to make up for lost time.

It was good.

As they parted, breathless and flushed, Charlotte marveled at the depth of emotion that swirled within her chest. *Was this love?* She had no experience in the matter. But she loved how it felt.

Alexander's fingers traced the curve of her cheek, his touch feather-light yet laden with unspoken meaning. "That was . . . nice," he murmured, his voice rich with admiration and a tender affection that sent her heart fluttering.

Charlotte leaned into his touch, reveling in the warmth of his presence. "I couldn't have done this without you, you know," she whispered breathlessly, her own words tinged with a newfound vulnerability. "Your faith in me has been a constant source of strength."

Alexander's expression softened, his eyes gleaming with an emotion that Charlotte found herself unable to name. "You underestimate your own fortitude, Charlotte," he replied, his voice low and intense. "This triumph is yours alone."

Reaching up, Charlotte covered his hand with her own, savoring the way their fingers intertwined. "Then let us share in this victory," she whispered, inching closer until she could feel the warmth of his breath caress her skin.

Alexander's gaze flickered to her lips, a silent invitation that sent a shiver of anticipation down her spine. Slowly, almost involuntarily, she leaned in, her eyes fluttering closed as his hand cupped her cheek, his touch sending sparks of electricity through her body once more. This time it was slow and purposeful. Their lips met in a tender, lingering kiss, all the longing and affection they had carefully hidden now laid bare.

When they finally parted once again, Charlotte felt a dizzying mix of exhilaration and trepidation. This was uncharted territory, a step beyond the boundaries of their professional relationship. Yet in Alexander's eyes, she saw a reflection of her own feelings - a deep, unwavering connection that transcended the constraints of propriety. What felt so good could not be wrong.

"Alexander..." she breathed, her voice barely above a whisper. She searched his face, seeking reassurance, permission, anything to anchor her in this moment of uncertainty.

His thumb grazed her cheek, a tender gesture that spoke volumes. "Charlotte," he murmured, his own voice tinged with a rare vulnerability. "I... I've wanted this for so long." His admission hung in the air, a confession that set her heart racing.

Emboldened by his words, Charlotte reached up, her fingers tracing the strong line of his jaw. "Then why did we wait?" she asked softly, her gaze locked with his.

Alexander's lips curved into a wistful smile. "Caution, I suppose. I didn't want to jeopardize what we had, what we were building together." His hand slid down to capture hers, squeezing gently. "But I can no longer deny what's in my heart."

Charlotte felt a surge of emotions within her, a heady mix of joy, apprehension, and a newfound sense of possibility. With a tremulous smile, she laced her fingers through his, savoring the warmth of his touch.

"Nor can I," she whispered, her eyes shining with a quiet determination. "I've come too far to let fear hold me back, not when..." Her voice trailed off, the unspoken words lingering between them.

Alexander's gaze softened, and he lifted her hand to press a reverent kiss against her fingertips. "Then let us forge ahead, together," he murmured, his words weighted with the promise of a future entwined.

Charlotte felt a flutter of excitement in her chest, the weight of their newfound intimacy both exhilarating and daunting. But as she stood there, with Alexander's unwavering support, she knew that whatever challenges lay ahead, they would face them side by side.

Charlotte was happy.

Chapter Twelve

Charlotte couldn't help but notice the folder sitting atop the stool in the kitchen. It had been left there, seemingly forgotten, since Alexander's last visit. Curiosity piqued, she found herself drawn to the unassuming envelope and papers inside, unable to resist the temptation to investigate.

Carefully, she eased the flap open and peeked inside. Her eyes widened as she caught a glimpse of the contents - pages filled with intricate diagrams and technical notes, all meticulously detailed. This was no ordinary document; it appeared to be something related to Project Arcanum. That part wasn't unusual, but the next letter caught her attention.

Charlotte's heart raced as she carefully extracted the papers, her gaze scanning quickly. A knot of unease formed in the pit of her stomach, mingling with a sense of violation at having invaded his privacy.

Just as she was about to return the papers, a particular phrase caught her eye, and she found herself unable to look away. The words seemed to leap off the page, stirring a whirlwind of emotions within her. Overwhelmed, Charlotte sank down onto the stool, her fingers trembling as she re-read the passage, desperate to make sense of its meaning. Wait. . . Was he working against her?

The envelope in Charlotte's hand suddenly felt heavy, the implications making her queasy.

For a moment, she hesitated, wanting to simply toss the letter aside and keep the illusions that had made her so happy. But she couldn't resist the truth. With trembling fingers, she continued. As she read more and more, the truth was excruciating. Alexander had never been interested in Project Arcanum or her desire to honor Mr. Pembroke's legacy. It was all a ruse, a means to further his family's ambitions of industrial dominance. And he had used her to do it.

The letter laid it all out. Maybe not in so many words, but close enough. How could she be expected to read anything else into it? And he had lied about his past! Or at least had neglected telling her. *There was always more to the story.*

Had he ever cared? At all?

Money and politics. That was always the way of the world.

Charlotte's fingers trembled as she re-read the letter, the words seeming to blur on the page. Shock and disbelief warred within her, threatening to overwhelm her senses.

The truth was undeniable - Alexander, the man she had come to care for, had not been honest about his identity or his intentions. Pembroke's legacy, the very project she had dedicated herself to, had merely been a means to an end for him and his powerful family.

Was that all she was, too?

She let the letter fall from her hands, its crisp edges fluttering to the floor. How could she have been so blind? The warning signs had been there all along, but she had chosen to ignore them, blinded by Alexander's charming facade and her own hopeful heart.

Anger flared within her, hot and consuming. To think that she had trusted him, had allowed herself to be drawn into his web of deception. Her jaw tightened, and she fought the urge to crumple the letter, to erase the evidence of his betrayal.

Instead, she bent down to retrieve the letter, her fingers smoothing the creases almost unconsciously. She needed to think, to make sense of this tangled web of lies and secrets. Pembroke had entrusted her with his life's work, and she would be damned if she let Alexander or his family take that away from her.

Determined, Charlotte straightened her spine, her eyes hardening with resolve. She would get to the bottom of this, no matter the cost. Pembroke's dream would not be shattered, not on her watch.

With a deep breath, she turned and made her way towards the library, where she could think in peace. The sound of the door closing behind her like a thud in the large room was fitting. She was angry. And hurt. She moved slowly through the aisles of books, normally a place that placated her, her fingers trailing over the covers of the leather-bound tomes nearly grabbing at many. She wanted to throw them at the window. Or through it.

Or at him.

The man she'd thought she might have a future with was nothing more than a lie, his interest in Project Arcanum a farce.

Jaw clenched, she smoothed the parchment against her skirts, as if the crisp whisper of paper could drown the roar of betrayal echoing through her mind.

She couldn't think. Her mind swam in and out of focus. Had he really only been interested in the technology? For his "investors"? Were they his family?

The oak floorboards creaking outside the room pierced Charlotte's anguished reverie as someone approached. She glanced up, blinking away the sheen of unshed tears, as the library door creaked open to admit Henrietta and an unexpected visitor.

"Miss Pembroke," Henrietta's voice was a gentle murmur, "Mr. Hawkins was most insistent on seeing you. I took the liberty of granting him entry."

Charlotte's lips parted, a faint rise of heat staining her cheeks as she beheld the journalist hovering in the doorway, his ever-present notepad clutched in hand. Instinctively, she made to shield the damning letter from his prying gaze, the parchment crinkling in her grasp.

Yet there was something in Geoffrey's expression that gave her pause – a glimmer of genuine concern amidst his characteristic inquisitiveness. In that fleeting moment, her customary reticence crumbled, the words tumbling forth in a torrent she could no longer restrain.

"He betrayed me, Mr. Hawkins," Charlotte confessed, her voice wavering with a rawness that surprised even herself. "Alexander Blythe was never the ally I believed him to be. This..." She raised the letter, acid burning the back of her throat. "This lays bare the truth of his deception. I don't know how else to see it."

Hawkins merely stared, his gaze solemn as he crossed the threshold, each footfall measured. Lowering himself into the adjacent armchair, he clasped his hands, the notepad resting idle in his lap.

"There's a lot at stake in Mr. Pembroke's achievement. *Your* achievement. Other parties would always have been interested," he murmured, his admission devoid of the sensationalism one might expect. "The Blythe name carries considerable weight in certain circles – circles where industry and ambition often eclipse matters . . . ah, of the heart."

"Of course it would be so," she said.

"Yet I've also witnessed the strength of your convictions, Miss Pembroke," he said, his gaze locking with hers. "You possess a resilience that transcends the fleeting deceptions of men driven by greed and power. From what I've come to know, I'll also add it's not always so simple. If I may, Alexander seems like one of the good ones. Just my humble opinion. But with all I've seen in my years? That man loves you."

Charlotte stared at the journalist, his words a confounding contrast to the damning evidence in her hands. *Loves me?* The very notion seemed preposterous in light of Alexander's duplicity. Yet there was an earnestness in Hawkins' gaze that gave her pause.

"If what you say is true, then why would he deceive me so?" she asked, her grip on the letter slackening. "Why keep his true identity a secret?"

Hawkins sighed, a veil of weariness passing over his features. "The ways of the world are not always simple, Miss Pembroke. There are forces at play that even the brightest of us can't always comprehend. But I've seen the way he looks at you. There is a tenderness there that belies mere ambition. My job is to ferret out the truth others hope no one sees."

Charlotte's brow furrowed, the turmoil within her warring between anger and the faintest glimmer of hope. "You truly believe he cares for me? Even after all this?"

"I do," Hawkins replied, his tone measured. "But the true test will be whether he is willing to sacrifice his own interests to prove it."

The door creaked open once more, and Henrietta's matronly figure reappeared, her spectacles perched precariously on the end of her nose. "Pardon the intrusion, but Mr. Blythe is here."

Charlotte's breath caught in her throat, the letter nearly slipping from her grasp. Steeling herself, she rose from the chair, her eyes narrowing. "Then by all means, Henrietta, show him in."

Moments later, Alexander Blythe stepped into the library, his usual poise and confidence tempered by a rare uncertainty. His gaze sought out Charlotte's, and she was struck by the vulnerability lurking beneath his meticulously cultivated facade.

"Charlotte," he began, his voice low and measured, as he took in the sight of what was in her hands. "I owe you an explanation. No, more than that – I owe you the truth."

Charlotte remained silent, her fingers flexing around the letter as she waited for him to continue.

Hawkins, too, observed the exchange with a pensive air, his notepad forgotten in his lap.

"The letter you hold," Alexander said, his eyes never leaving hers, "it does not tell the full story. I have... omitted certain details, not out of malice, but out of a need to protect those I care for. Including you."

Charlotte's grip on the letter tightened as Alexander's words hung in the air. Hawkins, ever the keen observer, remained silent, his gaze flickering between the two.

"Protect those you care for?" Charlotte echoed, her voice laced with a hint of skepticism. "Forgive me, *Mr. Blythe,* but your actions have done nothing but sow doubt and deception. How am I to believe anything you say?"

Alexander's brow furrowed, a flicker of pain crossing his features. "I understand your distrust, Charlotte. I've given you every reason to doubt my sincerity. But I beg you, allow me to explain. The truth is far more complex than what that letter suggests."

He took a moment, gathering his thoughts before continuing. "My family's name and connections have always been a burden, a weight that has shaped my life in ways I never wished. When I first came to your workshop, I was intrigued by your work, yes, but also by you. Your intelligence, your determination, your refusal to be cowed by the expectations of society – it was captivating."

Charlotte felt the sting of tears behind her eyes, but she blinked them away, unwilling to let her emotions betray her. "And so you decided to use me, to further your family's interests?"

"No, Charlotte, never that." Alexander shook his head vehemently. "I came to genuinely assist you, to see Pembroke's legacy through. But I could not risk revealing my true identity, not when it could jeopardize everything you've worked for. My family's intentions for what they wanted here were never mine."

"How dare you say—"

Hawkins cleared his throat, drawing their attention. "If I may interject, Miss Pembroke?" At Charlotte's hesitation, he continued, "It seems there are layers to this narrative that we have yet to uncover. Perhaps it would be wise to hear Mr. Blythe out, to understand the full context of his actions."

Charlotte's gaze darted between the two men, torn between her wounded pride and a glimmer of curiosity. Finally, she sighed, her shoulders sagging with the weight of her doubts. "Very well. I'm listening."

Alexander's posture relaxed slightly, relief flickering across his features. "Thank you, Charlotte. I know I have much to explain, but I hope you'll understand that my intentions, however misguided they may have seemed, were never to hurt you."

"Family. Trust. Hurt... What else can you have expected to take from me?" She didn't even know what she was saying anymore. *I'm just so tired. Tired of the long days, the setbacks, the lack of knowing who has my best interests...*

"Just . . . hear me out. Please." Alexander met Charlotte's gaze, his expression earnest. "I care for you, Charlotte, more than you know. But my family's name and legacy have always cast a long shadow. When I first came to your workshop, I was drawn to your work, yes, but also to you. Your brilliance, your determination - it captivated me."

He paused, running a hand through his hair. "I wanted to help you, to see Pembroke's dream realized. But I couldn't risk revealing my true identity, not when it could threaten everything you've built. I didn't think you'd trust me."

Charlotte's grip on the letter tightened, her brows knitting together. "And so you decided deceit was the answer?"

"Not deceit, Charlotte," Alexander said, his voice low. "Protection. My family's ambitions have always been at odds with Pembroke's work. I couldn't allow them to use me to undermine your achievements."

Hawkins leaned forward, his gaze keen. "So you sought to walk a delicate line - assisting Miss

Pembroke while shielding her from your family's machinations."

Alexander nodded, his eyes never leaving Charlotte's. "Yes, precisely. I know it was a risk, but I..." He hesitated, a hint of vulnerability seeping into his expression. "I couldn't bear the thought of losing you."

Charlotte felt the weight of his words settle upon her, the turmoil within her subsiding slightly. Glancing down at the letter in her hands, she traced the elegant script, her mind racing.

"If what you say is true," she began slowly, "then why keep your true identity a secret? Surely there was another way to protect me and his legacy."

Alexander sighed, a veil of weariness passing over his features. "I wanted to, Charlotte, believe me. But my family... they have their ways of exerting influence, of manipulating those who threaten their interests. I couldn't risk them discovering my ... personal, connection to you, not when so much was at stake."

Hawkins shifted in his chair, his gaze thoughtful. "And yet, you're here now, revealing the truth. What changed?" The man loved a good story, and he was getting one, that was for certain.

Alexander's eyes flickered with a steely resolve. "I realized that the risk of losing you was far greater than any threat my family could pose. I couldn't bear the thought of you thinking me a heartless opportunist, not when my feelings for you are so genuine."

Charlotte felt her breath catch in her throat, the letter trembling in her hands. "Your feelings..." She paused, the weight of his words sinking in. "You mean to say ... well, what *do* you mean to say?"

He took a deep breath, and Charlotte saw something in him she hadn't seen before. She saw the pain of a man who had been burdened by the weight of his family name, a man who had carried it like a shackle.

"Look, when I first approached you, Charlotte, I will not lie, my intentions were... complicated," he admitted, keeping eye contact. "This project, this...*revolution*, the potential it had for revolutionizing industry, was something I could not pass up."

Charlotte felt a sting of betrayal run through her, the memory of her trust being broken. But, despite her reservations, she could still see the honesty in Alexander's eyes. "And?"

"But something happened in that room, Charlotte. I saw it – and I saw you. You care about Pembroke's dream, and that made me begin to look at things differently."

He reached out a hand to her, stopping just short of touching her. "You showed me that I was wrong to dismiss your work. You showed me that what you were doing was important, and that it wasn't the same goals that had driven my family members to their actions."

Charlotte felt a shiver run through her. Could it be that the two of them had formed some kind of connection that had nothing to do with the initial reasons they had been thrown together?

"I have come to you now, Charlotte, with no pretense. I care about you. And I care about your work. If you would have me, I would like to start anew, with both of our goals aligned, and with no mention of what has happened in the past. I care about *you,* and what you and I …" he glanced at Hawkins, "…what you and I have shared. And *can* share. If you'll let me."

The entire room seemed to have gone silent. The gears had stopped, as if they were waiting to see what Charlotte would do. Would she be able to forgive Alexander for what he had done, or was there no chance of her ever trusting him again?

"I . . . *need* you. I think you understand. Can you forgive my transgressions? I wasn't honest. At first. But Charlotte…"

She listened. Her heart opened a little more. *But he'd come under false pretenses.* His family was after Mr. Pembroke's legacy. But she knew he was being genuine. At least now. They'd shared so many moments together, so many long days and late nights. *That kiss…* The *kiss…*

What to do?

After Alexander had left, Charlotte returned to her room and stood in front of the mirror, looking at the woman she had become. In the dim light, she could see the fire in her eyes. She had been oppressed by the expectations of society for far too long. She was a woman of intelligence and perseverance, and now she was determined to use those traits to their fullest. Alexander had been her catalyst, and now she was ready.

With a steadying breath, Charlotte straightened her posture, squaring her shoulders as she regarded her reflection anew. Gone was the wide-eyed naivete that had once defined her, replaced by the unflinching poise of a woman who had stared into the abyss of betrayal and emerged emboldened.

A faint smile tugged at the corners of her lips, suffusing her demeanor with a quiet confidence that belied the emotional tempest still roiling beneath the surface. She would see Project Arcanum through to its rightful fruition – with or without Alexander's aid, her resolve now as immutable as the gleaming gears and cogs that constituted her life's work.

In this moment, suspended between past and future, the weight of her decision seemed to reverberate through the hallowed space.

To accept Alexander's proposal and move forward with a partnership that was equal parts trust and distrust...or to deny his offer and continue to pursue her vision without the burden of his previous deceit. She was at a crossroads now, where the echoes of her mentor's teachings mixed with her own determination.

But Charlotte knew she was already in too deep. She cared for him.

A lot.

Chapter Thirteen

The Great Exhibition loomed large in front of her, and now it was about replicating her work to prove its viability. Lives would be made and ruined at this event, all based on scientific replication.

She could duplicate the progress they'd made. At least, that was the plan, and it seemed to be feasible, even if at a faster rate.

Limitless energy. Or nearabouts, anyway. But that was the story that had taken ahold of the science world. Untold riches, said many. But she wasn't interested in any of that.

Just the work it provides your mind and fingers, she thought to herself. *That's your love, your passion.*

As the days tick by and the Great Exhibition demonstration came ever closer, Charlotte was feverishly working to replicate her project—*his* project. The pressure mounted with each passing hour, her focus intense and her determination unwavering.

"Just a little more," she murmured, her fingers nimble and precise as she coaxed the components into place. This was her chance to honor Pembroke's legacy, to show the world the incredible potential of his vision.

During a critical test run, a vital component suddenly failed, sparking a cascade of problems that rapidly spiraled out of control. Charlotte watched in dismay as the prototype shuddered and began to smoke, the intricate dance of machinery grinding to a halt.

"No, no, no!" she cried, rushing to shut down the system before further damage could be done. Her heart pounded in her ears as she surveyed the damage, her mind racing to find a solution.

The failure threatened to jeopardize her chances of a successful presentation at the Exhibition. Charlotte felt a wave of panic wash over her, but she refused to let it consume her. Pembroke had entrusted her with this project, and she would be damned if she let it all fall apart now.

Steeling her nerves, Charlotte set to work, her hands moving with a renewed sense of urgency as she began to disassemble the prototype, searching for the root cause of the malfunction. The ticking clock echoed in her mind, spurring her on even as fatigue threatened to overtake her.

The workshop door creaked open, and Alexander entered, his brow furrowed with concern. He approached Charlotte, who stood hunched over the dismantled prototype, her face etched with frustration.

"Charlotte," he said, his voice laced with worry. "What happened? Let me help you."

At 20 years old, Charlotte wasn't supposed to be this intense, this driven. The looming pressure of the Great Exhibition had taken its toll.

"I've got this," she said, her tone clipped. "I don't need your help."

Alexander's brow furrowed deeper, and he took a step closer. "Please, Charlotte. I only want to assist you. We're in this together, remember?"

Together. The word echoed in Charlotte's mind, stirring a flurry of emotions. She yearned for his support, his unwavering belief in her abilities. But it was all too much. She'd eaten little, slept even less.

Swallowing her pride, she met his gaze, her eyes pleading. "I just... I need to figure this out on my own. I have to prove I can do this."

Alexander nodded slowly, understanding dawning on his features. "I know. But you don't have to shoulder this burden alone. Let me be your ally, Charlotte. Let me help you."

The sincerity in his words tugged at her heart, and for a moment, Charlotte allowed herself to believe in his sincerity. Yet, the echoes of past deceptions still whispered in the back of her mind, a constant reminder of the fragility of her trust.

Exhaling a deep breath, she turned back to the prototype, her fingers resuming their careful work. "Okay," she conceded, her voice barely above a whisper. "But I'm leading this. I can't afford any more mistakes."

Over the next few days, Thomas Keating subtly sowed seeds of doubt among Charlotte's supporters. With an air of feigned concern, he suggested that perhaps Alexander may be behind the repeated sabotage attempts, heightening the tension and drama. The last year had seen plenty. Some coincidence, surely, others more blatant. And then there were the stories circulated to cast shadows on her work in the press. Thankfully, Geoffrey was helping his best there.

"I hate to be the one to say this," Keating said innocently to Henrietta one afternoon, his brow furrowed in an expression of worry, "but have you considered the possibility that Mr. Blythe may not be as genuine as he seems? After all, the timing of these setbacks is quite curious, is it not?"

Henrietta frowned, her loyalty to Alexander at odds with the niggling doubts Keating's words had planted in her mind. "I find that hard to believe. Mr. Blythe has been nothing but helpful and supportive of

Charlotte's work. Even more so, now. He stands to lose if she fails."

Keating nodded solemnly. "Maybe. But my understanding is that he didn't exactly represent himself honestly. I understand your hesitation, but I feel it's only fair to consider all possibilities. Charlotte has worked so hard, and I would hate to see her efforts undermined by someone she has come to trust. Mr. Pembroke and I were close, I'm sure he'd feel the same way."

Henrietta's lips pressed into a thin line, her eyes narrowing as she processed Keating's insinuations. The very idea of Alexander betraying Charlotte's trust was unthinkable, and yet, a seed of doubt had been sown.

The next evening, overwhelmed by the stress and uncertainty, Charlotte retreated to the solace of Pembroke's study. Henrietta found her there, eyes red from tears, and gently coaxed her to share her worries.

"My dear child, what troubles you so?" Henrietta asked, her voice soft and soothing as she placed a comforting hand on Charlotte's shoulder.

Charlotte sniffed, her gaze downcast. "I don't know what to think anymore, Henrietta. The setbacks, the sabotage... and now Keating is suggesting that even Alexander may be involved." She shook her head, a fresh wave of anguish washing over her. "I never wanted any of this. Never. Just. . . just a life doing what I love. I feel so guilty. I'm doing all this to thank Mr. . . to thank Richard for taking me in. Even after everything I've learned, knowing he kept so much from me, I just want to do his legacy honour. I know he wanted the best for me. But I'm over my head in all this."

"Maybe," she started. "Maybe not. But he believed in you. *You* believed in you, once. You can again."

"But there's so much involved! This isn't like putting a watch back together at the orphanage. Livelihood's are at stake. Careers, fortunes, even. Who can I trust anymore?"

Henrietta's expression softened with empathy. "Oh, Charlotte, I can only imagine how difficult this must be for you. But you mustn't lose faith, my dear. Mr. Blythe has shown himself to be a true friend to you, and I cannot believe he would betray that trust."

Charlotte looked up, her eyes pleading. "But what if Keating is right? What if Alexander is somehow involved in all the things that keep holding everything back? I don't think I could bear it."

Henrietta pulled Charlotte into a warm embrace, stroking her hair gently. "Hush now, child. In times of trouble, it's important to hold fast to those who have proven themselves worthy of our trust." She paused, a wistful smile tugging at her lips. "Your mentor, Mr. Pembroke, always saw the best in people. Perhaps it's time to remember that you do too. I know you do."

Charlotte's shoulders relaxed, and she nodded, her resolve slowly beginning to rebuild. In the comfort of Henrietta's presence, she found the strength to face the challenges ahead.

Charlotte paced anxiously in Pembroke's study, her mind whirling with conflicting thoughts and emotions. The weight of responsibility, the sting of betrayal, and the dread of losing Alexander's trust all threatened to overwhelm her.

No more!

She needed answers, now. *Put things I can't control to rest, one way or another.*

Straightening her shoulders, she strode to the workshop, determined to confront Alexander and uncover the truth.

"Alexander," she called out, her voice wavering slightly. "I... I need to speak with you."

Alexander looked up, his expression one of concern. "Charlotte, what is it? Is everything alright?" He walked over to her so they were alone.

Charlotte took a deep breath, her gaze locking with his. "No, everything is not alright. I've been... hearing things. Whispers about you, about your involvement in the sabotage attempts. If that's what they are. Who can know what's sabotage, what's accident, what's natural setbacks… Who knows anything anymore when it comes to this whole thing?" She paused, her eyes searching his face. "But I need to know the truth,

Alexander. I need to know if I can trust you. Right here, right now. Your past... fine. Whatever. But are you with me or not?"

Alexander's brow furrowed, and he took a step closer to her. "Charlotte, what on earth are you talking about? I would never do anything to sabotage your work. You know that."

"Do I?" Charlotte's voice cracked, the weight of her exhaustion and uncertainty seeping through. "I thought I knew a lot of things, but now I'm not so sure. The rumors, the setbacks... it's all just become too much."

She ran a hand through her hair, her eyes brimming with unshed tears. "I'm so tired, Alexander. Tired of fighting, tired of doubting everyone around me. I just want to... I just want to do what Mr. Pembroke asked of me. To honor his legacy. He chose me, trusted me! But I can't do that if I can't trust the people I've come to care about."

Her gaze met his, a silent plea for reassurance. "Please, Alexander. Tell me the truth. I need to know if I can trust you, or if I'm just setting myself up for more heartbreak. Not that would tell me if you have some grand, secret plan to ... to whatever. I dunno."

Alexander's expression softened, and he reached out to gently take her hand. "Charlotte, I understand your doubts, and I don't blame you for them. After all that you've been through, it's only natural to be wary. But I want you to know, with every fiber of my being, that I would never, ever do anything to jeopardize your work or your trust."

He squeezed her hand, his eyes searching hers. "From the moment I met you, I've been in awe of your brilliance, your determination, and your unwavering commitment to honoring Mr. Pembroke's legacy. I told you that, and I mean it. That is why I'm here, Charlotte. To support you, to help you in any way I can."

Charlotte felt the tension in her shoulders begin to ease as Alexander's words sank in. "But... the rumors, the sabotage. How can I be sure you're not involved?"

Alexander shook his head slowly. "I can't control the rumors, Charlotte, but I can assure you that I have had no part in the sabotage attempts. In fact, I've been working tirelessly to try and uncover the source of these setbacks, to protect your work and your dreams."

He paused, his gaze intense. "You have to believe me, Charlotte. I would never do anything to betray your trust. You... you mean too much to me. What we have … it's real. For me, and I know it is for you."

Charlotte's breath caught in her throat, the raw emotion in his words stirring something deep within her. She searched his face, a glimmer of hope igniting in her heart.

"Alexander, I..." She hesitated, her fingers tightening around his. "I want to believe you. I want to trust you. But I'm... I'm so afraid of being hurt again. I'm so tired."

Alexander nodded, his thumb gently caressing the back of her hand. "I know, Charlotte. I know. But I promise you, I will do everything in my power to prove my loyalty and my devotion to you. Whatever it takes."

She collapsed then, into his chest. She didn't care anymore. She would trust him. Because she wanted to, and she did. Keating had gotten to her, and perhaps that's what he wanted. If he was responsible for the rest, there would be hell to pay.

But for now, she was glad to be in Alexander's arms.

Chapter Fourteen

A week before the Great Exhibition, the Pembroke workshop buzzed with a frenetic energy. Charlotte Pembroke stood before the prototype, her brow furrowed in deep concentration as she meticulously checked each intricate component. Alexander Blythe stood at her side, his gaze filled with a quiet admiration as he watched her work.

"I still can't believe we made it this far without any further setbacks," Charlotte murmured. "It feels too good to be true."

Alexander reached out and gently squeezed her hand, his touch sending a familiar flutter through Charlotte's chest. "You've worked so hard, Charlotte. Pembroke would be proud to see how far you've come."

She met his warm gaze, a small smile tugging at the corners of her lips. "Honestly, I couldn't have done it without you. Your support and guidance have meant everything to me. Thank you."

They lapsed into a comfortable silence, the only sound the gentle whir of the machinery they had poured their hearts and souls into. Charlotte felt a weight lift from her shoulders, the constant worry and doubt that had plagued her in recent months finally starting to subside.

As the afternoon wore on, Henrietta Clarke, the Pembroke household's warm and steadfast housekeeper, poked her head into the workshop. "Charlotte, dear, I'm going out for the afternoon. Will you two be alright on your own?"

Charlotte glanced at Alexander, a mischievous glint in her intelligent eyes. "I think we can manage, Henrietta. Enjoy your outing. Wait, is this a date?" She'd noticed makeup on her face.

Henrietta smiled, then eyed them both knowingly before retreating, leaving Charlotte and Alexander alone in the quiet sanctuary of the Pembroke workshop.

Alexander stepped closer, his hand brushing against Charlotte's arm in a feather-light caress. "Well. Alone at last," he murmured, his voice low and full of promise.

Charlotte felt a familiar flutter in her chest as she met his gaze, her heart racing with a mixture of anticipation and trepidation. "It would appear so." She hesitated for a moment, then reached up to trace the strong line of his jaw, marvelling at the way his features seemed to soften under her touch. "I'm glad we've been able to move past the doubts and focus on what's truly important."

"As am I," Alexander said, his hand coming to rest on her slender waist, drawing her closer. "It's rather peaceful, now, isn't it? Despite the end of the journey?"

"Peaceful. Hmm. . . yes. And I'm grateful to have found that peace with you," she murmured, her voice barely above a whisper. Closing the distance between them, she allowed herself to be enveloped in his embrace, the familiar scent of him washing over her like a balm. In his arms, she felt a sense of belonging, a profound connection that transcended the challenges they had faced. For now, in this quiet moment, the world seemed to fade away, leaving only the two of them and the promise of a brighter tomorrow. She could never define what they had, what they had done before. The kisses. The closeness.

It only bothered her a little, though. Charlotte liked him, liked how he made her feel.

Slowly, he leaned in, his lips brushing against hers in a tender, achingly gentle kiss. Charlotte sighed, melting into his warm embrace as the kiss deepened, all the tension and worry of the past few months seeming to melt away, replaced by a sense of safety and belonging that she had never known before.

When they finally parted, both breathless and flushed, Charlotte rested her forehead against his, savouring the closeness.

They stood there, wrapped in each other's arms, savoring the precious moment of solitude.

What *did* they have? What were they? They'd never spoken about it, but for now, she was okay with it. For now.

The day of the Great Exhibition dawned bright and clear, the air electric with anticipation. Charlotte Pembroke stood backstage, the weight of the task ahead settling heavily upon her shoulders. Years of meticulous work, of pushing past obstacles and self-doubt, had led to this moment.

She took a deep breath, willing her trembling hands to steady. Charlotte cast one final glance at the elegant prototype of Project Arcanum, its complex and intricate mechanisms a testament to her mentor's vision and her own unwavering dedication.

Straightening her spine, Charlotte stepped out onto the stage, her expression resolute. The vast exhibition hall was packed to the brim, a sea of curious faces turned towards her. She scanned the crowd, her gaze briefly meeting Alexander's, who stood amongst the throng, offering her an encouraging nod. There were still some faces that clearly hadn't expected a woman to be on stage; they obviously hadn't been paying attention in recent months to their own world happenings. Either way, she was ready.

"Ladies and gentlemen," Charlotte began, her clear voice carrying across the space, "I am honoured to present to you today the culmination of a lifetime of work – Project Arcanum."

As she walked the audience through the technical details of the prototype, Charlotte felt a surge of confidence. The years of apprenticeship under Pembroke's tutelage, the countless hours spent hunched over blueprints and calibrating delicate mechanisms, had all led to this moment. Gone was the timid, shy girl from the orphanage, replaced by a radiant, assured woman who commanded the room with her mastery of the subject matter.

Charlotte's fingers danced across the controls, and the prototype thrummed to life. The audience collectively held their breath as the machine began to move, its gears turning with a mesmerizing precision. She narrated the intricate processes, explaining how the innovative electromagnetic principles that drove the machine could revolutionize the fields of power generation, transportation, and potentially so much more.

Amidst the rapt silence, the prototype performed its tasks flawlessly, eliciting gasps of wonder and applause from the captivated onlookers. Charlotte's heart soared, the hard-won triumph of this moment eclipsing the challenges she had faced along the way.

In that instant, she was no longer the orphan girl who had once dreamed of a better life beyond the bleak walls of Hawthornfield. She was Charlotte Pembroke, engineer extraordinaire, the rightful heir to Pembroke's legacy, and a trailblazer in her own right. The transformation was palpable, and the audience seemed to sense it.

The thunderous applause echoed through the grand exhibition hall, filling Charlotte with a profound sense of pride and vindication. As the crowd celebrated her triumph, a delegation of prestigious investors and industrialists approached, eager to discuss the future development of Project Arcanum.

"Magnificent work, my dear!" exclaimed Lord Mercer, his weathered face alight with genuine admiration. "Pembroke would be most proud to see his legacy carried on in such a remarkable fashion."

Charlotte felt a flush of warmth spread across her cheeks. "Thank you, my lord. I merely aimed to honour his vision to the best of my abilities."

"And you have succeeded beyond measure," Mercer replied, his gaze shifting to include Alexander, who stood beside Charlotte, his expression radiating quiet pride. "You both have quite a remarkable achievement on your hands. I, for one, would be most interested in supporting the continued advancement of this project."

Alexander stepped forward, his diplomatic charm on full display. "We would be honoured to discuss the possibilities with you and your esteemed colleagues, my lord. Project Arcanum has the potential to revolutionize so many industries."

As the group of investors began to surround Charlotte and Alexander, a sudden commotion drew everyone's attention. Thomas Keating, his usually composed demeanour shattered, pushed his way through the crowd, his face twisted with rage.

"This is an outrage!" Keating shouted, his voice carrying across the hall. "That device is my rightful creation, not hers!" He pointed an accusatory finger at Charlotte, his eyes wild with jealousy.

Charlotte felt a chill run down her spine as Keating's tirade continued, the man's carefully cultivated mask of civility crumbling away to reveal the true depths of his bitterness and resentment.

"How dare you, a woman, steal the results of my work!" Keating spat, "Pembroke should never have left his legacy to the likes of you. You don't belong here. You should be back in your home, tending to your sewing and your chores."

Alexander stepped forward, his stance protective as he placed himself between Keating and Charlotte. "That's quite enough, Keating. Your baseless accusations hold no merit. Charlotte has earned her place through her exceptional skills and hard work."

Keating's eyes narrowed, his gaze darting between Charlotte and Alexander. "Oh, I see how it is. You've both conspired to rob me of what is rightfully mine. Well, I won't stand for it. That should be *my* success!" He let out a deranged laugh, his composure slipping further. "I was the one who sabotaged your precious project, you know. I couldn't bear to see Pembroke's legacy tarnished by the hands of a woman!"

The crowd erupted in a collective gasp, the revelation of Keating's treachery stunning them into silence. Charlotte felt a surge of vindication, her suspicions about the mysterious setbacks finally confirmed. Alexander's grip on her arm tightened, his expression hardening as he realized the depths of Keating's betrayal.

"You admit to it?" Alexander's voice was low and dangerous. "Do you have any idea of the consequences you now face?"

Keating's eyes widened as he seemed to comprehend the gravity of his own admission. "I-I..." he stammered, his bravado crumbling. Keating's face contorted in anguish as the weight of his actions crashed down upon him. "This cannot be!" he cried, his voice laced with despair. The prospect of his hard-earned career and carefully cultivated reputation being utterly destroyed filled him with a sense of overwhelming dread.

The investors and bystanders watched, transfixed, as Keating's desperate attempts to salvage his position unravelled before their eyes. Charlotte felt a sense of vindication wash over her, the weight of Keating's treachery finally lifted from her shoulders.

In the midst of the commotion, several familiar faces from the Pembroke workshop pushed through the crowd, their expressions ranging from begrudging respect to genuine admiration. One of the senior engineers, a gruff-looking man, stepped forward and placed a weathered hand on Charlotte's shoulder.

"Well done, lass," he said gruffly, a glimmer of pride in his eyes. "Pembroke would be proud to see how you've carried on his legacy."

Charlotte's heart swelled with a surge of emotion at the unexpected support from the engineer. His hand on her shoulder conveyed a warmth and pride that she hadn't expected, causing her eyes to shine with grateful tears. As Keating was forcibly escorted from the premises, the cloud of suspicion and doubt that had hung over Charlotte for so long finally lifted, replaced by a renewed sense of purpose and belonging. She stood a little taller, the weight of Keating's treachery no longer burdening her. This was her moment of vindication, a validation of all the hard work and determination she had poured into her craft. A small, triumphant smile tugged at the corners of her lips as she watched Keating's desperate attempts to salvage his position unravel before their eyes, yelling and looking around for any support.

He had none.

Rightfully so.

It was a relief, in so many ways. Her work was vindicated, *she* was vindicated.

And so was Alexander.

Truly, the day had been a success. People wanted to talk to her; the crowd was thick. It was good.

But all she wanted to do was sleep.

But it was a good day, she thought, allowing herself a small smile.

Chapter Fifteen

The morning light filtered through the large windows, casting a warm glow over Charlotte's office - the very space where she had spent countless hours under Pembroke's tutelage. She leaned back in the chair, running her fingers along the smooth surface of the desk as a sense of contentment washed over her.

A gentle rap on the door preceded Henrietta's entrance, her arms laden with a stack of letters and parcels. "More well-wishes and offers pouring in from all corners, my dear," she said, depositing the bundle atop the already crowded desk.

Charlotte let out a soft chuckle, her gaze sweeping over the various envelopes bearing the crests of prestigious institutions and industrialists. "It's been a whirlwind since the Exhibition, hasn't it?"

Henrietta nodded sagely. "Indeed, though Mr. Blythe has been most insistent that I turn away any unannounced visitors for the time being. He believes you deserve a respite after all your hard work."

A faint blush crept onto Charlotte's cheeks at the mention of Alexander's thoughtfulness. "He needn't worry so. A bit of busyness does me good, keeps my mind active."

"Well, you know my thoughts on the matter," Henrietta said with a wink. "Though I dare say we both could use a moment to catch our breaths."

Charlotte gestured for her old friend to take a seat nearby. "Tell me, how fare things between you and Charles these days?"

Henrietta's eyes twinkled with a rare mischievousness. "Oh, you know us old folks. We find our stolen moments where we can - a lingering touch here, a cheeky wink there." She leaned in conspiratorially. "Between you and me, the man still manages to make my heart flutter like a schoolgirl's. Food isn't all he's cookin'."

Laughter bubbled forth from Charlotte's lips at Henrietta's candor. "Is that so? Well, in that case, perhaps it's time I insisted you both take up permanent residence here at the estate. No more of this coming and going business."

Henrietta's expression melted into one of unabashed delight. "You're too kind, my dear. I'll broach the subject with Charles straight away."

As their laughter intermingled, Charlotte couldn't help but bask in the moment - a small respite amidst the whirlwind, a chance to revel in the simple joys of friendship and camaraderie. For now, the accolades and offers could wait; she had all she needed right here.

Later that afternoon, as Charlotte prepared to head out for a restorative walk, a familiar knock sounded at the workshop door. She looked up from the delicate piece of machinery she had been tinkering with and smiled, recognising the distinct cadence.

"Come in, Mr. Hawkins," she called, quickly wiping the grease from her fingers.

The door swung open, and the tall, lanky figure of the journalist strode in, his ever-present notebook tucked into the breast pocket of his waistcoat. "Miss Pembroke," he greeted with a warm smile, "or should I say, the toast of London?"

Charlotte felt a flush creep up her neck at his words. "Please, call me Charlotte. And I hardly think I'm the toast of London, Mr. Hawkins."

Hawkins chuckled, his spectacles glinting in the afternoon light. "Ah, but that's where you're mistaken, my dear. Your triumph at the Great Exhibition has set tongues wagging all across the city." He produced a freshly printed newspaper from behind his back. "In fact, I've written a rather extensive piece about you and your remarkable achievements, especially for a—"

"A woman?" she asked, coyly.

"No, for a person so young such as yourself," he responded, smiling. "Although you're making waves with that part too."

Charlotte took the newspaper, her fingers tracing the bold headline that proclaimed her as "Britain's Rising Engineering Star." Skimming the article, she was struck by the depth of Hawkins' research and the reverence with which he described her work on Project Arcanum.

"Mr. Hawkins, I don't know what to say," she murmured, her voice thick with emotion. "This is... quite extraordinary."

Hawkins waved a hand dismissively. "Nonsense, my dear. You've more than earned this recognition. And please, call me Geoffrey. After all, I feel as though I've come to know you quite well through my investigations."

Charlotte nodded, setting the newspaper aside and meeting his gaze. "In that case, thank you, Geoffrey. Your support and belief in me have meant a great deal, especially in those early days when so many doubted my abilities."

"Ah, but I never doubted you, Charlotte," Geoffrey said, his expression softening. "From the moment I first witnessed your passion and brilliance, I knew you were destined for greatness. And now, the world shall know it as well."

Charlotte felt a surge of pride, tempered by a touch of humility. "I couldn't have done it without Mr.

Pembroke's guidance and the assistance of my friends. This is as much their triumph as it is mine."

Geoffrey nodded knowingly. "Indeed, and I've made sure to give credit where it's due. However, it is your vision and determination that have truly brought this marvel to life. You should be exceedingly proud of yourself."

Charlotte offered him a genuine smile. "I am, Geoffrey. Truly, I am. And I have you to thank, in no small part, for helping me to see that."

"Well, then, I suppose a congratulatory toast is in order," Geoffrey said, producing a small flask from his coat pocket. "I may have taken the liberty of procuring a bit of brandy for the occasion."

Charlotte let out a delighted laugh. "How thoughtful of you. I believe I could use a moment of celebration, if you don't mind the company of a rather grease-stained engineer."

"My dear Charlotte," Geoffrey replied, pouring the amber liquid into a pair of glasses, "I wouldn't have it any other way."

The gentle breeze carried the scent of freshly bloomed flowers as Charlotte stepped out into the sunlit day, her mind abuzz with the flurry of offers and letters that had consumed her morning. Tucking a stray lock of hair behind her ear, she made her way towards the park, eager to meet Alexander.

As she strolled along the gravel path, the weight of Pembroke's legacy and her own uncertain origins seemed to linger in the back of her mind, like a persistent whisper. Charlotte knew that the accolades and opportunities that had come her way were a testament to the hard work and determination she had poured into honoring her mentor's vision, but they also served as a constant reminder of the immense responsibility she now bore.

Rounding the familiar corner, she spotted Alexander's tall, imposing figure standing beneath the shade of a towering oak tree. A smile tugged at the corners of her lips as she quickened her pace, and he turned to greet her, his own expression radiating a welcoming warmth.

"Charlotte," he said, his voice low and measured, "I'm glad you could join me. You look positively radiant today."

She felt a faint blush creep across her cheeks at his compliment. "Thank you, Alexander. It's been a rather eventful morning, to say the least."

Alexander nodded, his gaze settling on her face with a curious intensity. "I can only imagine. The offers and invitations must be pouring in after your triumph at the Exhibition. You deserve the attention. Enjoy it."

Charlotte fell into step beside him as they began to stroll through the park, the dappled sunlight filtering through the trees. "Indeed, it's been rather overwhelming. I've received letters from prestigious universities, industrialists, and even a few foreign dignitaries, all eager to be associated with the work we did."

Alexander's brow furrowed slightly. "And how do you feel about all of this, Charlotte? I know the weight of Pembroke's legacy must weigh heavily upon you."

"It's . . . overwhelming. I'm twenty." She let out a soft sigh, her fingers tracing the delicate petals of a nearby flower. "I'd be lying if I said it didn't trouble me, Alexander. Pembroke's vision was so personal, so integral to who he was, and now the responsibility of honoring that has fallen squarely upon my shoulders. Feels like I haven't stopped working since I came to live with him. Would he approve? Be proud? Did I do his legacy right?"

"You've more than proven yourself worthy of that mantle, Charlotte," Alexander said, his voice reassuring. "Pembroke saw something in you, something extraordinary, and you've done him proud, most certainly. You should be confident in your abilities to carry on his work. He loved you, that is also certain. But yes," he said, looking up, taking in the sights around him. "You should take time for yourself, now."

Charlotte nodded, appreciating the sentiment behind his words, but a hint of uncertainty still lingered in her expression. "I know, and I am grateful for the opportunities that have presented themselves. But I can't help but wonder about my own place in all of this. Who was I, truly, before Pembroke took me in?"

Alexander reached out, gently placing his hand on her arm. "Whatever your origins, Charlotte, they don't define you. Pembroke saw the brilliance in you, the passion and determination that made you the woman you are today. That is what truly matters."

She met his gaze, finding solace in the steady warmth of his eyes. "You're right, of course. I shouldn't let these doubts consume me. Pembroke believed in me, and that is what I must hold onto."

"Precisely," Alexander said, his lips curving into a reassuring smile. "And you have allies, Charlotte – people who believe in you and will support you as you navigate this new chapter. You need not shoulder this burden alone."

Charlotte felt a surge of gratitude towards this man who had become such an integral part of her life. "I don't know what I would do without your steadfast guidance. Your understanding. And of course, your pretty eyes."

Alexander laughed, and they continued their stroll, the verdant landscape and the gentle breeze providing a soothing backdrop to their conversation. Charlotte allowed herself to enjoy the tranquility of the moment, savoring the respite from the constant whirlwind of obligations and expectations that had come to define her days.

As they neared the edge of the park, Charlotte turned to Alexander, her expression thoughtful. "I must admit, I'm still grappling with the weight of it all, these past few years, and my own uncertainties about my past. But with you by my side, I feel I can face whatever challenges lie ahead. You will . . . still be by my side, right?" She couldn't hide the uncertainty in her voice.

He leaned in then, his expression softening as he gazed into her eyes. "Charlotte, there's something I need to tell you."

She felt her heartbeat quicken, an anticipatory flutter in her chest as she held his gaze. "Yes?"

He took a deep breath, seeming to steel himself before speaking. "I...I've fallen in love with you." His voice was low, tinged with a vulnerability she had rarely seen from him.

Charlotte felt a warmth blossom within her, mingling with the swirl of emotions she had been grappling with. "Alexander..."

He continued, his words tumbling forth with an uncharacteristic urgency. "From the moment I first met you, I was captivated by your brilliance, your resilience, and your unwavering dedication to everything important to you. But it's so much more than that. You've become...everything to me."

Charlotte felt a lump forming in her throat, her eyes shining with unshed tears. "I don't know what to say..."

Alexander lifted his free hand to gently caress her cheek. "You don't have to say anything, Charlotte. I know the weight you carry, the uncertainties you face. But I want you to know that I will be by your side, no matter what. I've made sacrifices, hidden truths, all to ensure your safety and the success of Pembroke's work. Because you, Charlotte, are worth fighting for."

The sincerity in his voice, the vulnerability she saw reflected in his eyes, stirred something deep within her. She had always been drawn to Alexander, his quiet strength and unwavering support a constant source of comfort. Not to mention their stolen moments alone. But now, in this moment, she realized the depths of her own feelings for him. The reality of where it all came from. They were more than just moments for her, too.

"Alexander, I..." She faltered, her hand covering his as it rested against her cheek. "I didn't know. I knew there was something special between us, but I never dared to hope..." Her voice trailed off, the words catching in her throat.

He leaned in closer, his forehead gently touching hers. "Hope, Charlotte. That's all I ask. Let me be with you. Now, always…"

Charlotte closed her eyes, savoring the intimacy of the moment, the weight of his words settling over her.

In the span of a heartbeat, her own doubts and fears seemed to melt away, replaced by a profound sense of trust and affection for the man before her.

"You have my heart, Alexander," she whispered, her fingers entwining with his. "You have me."

A smile spread across his features, the tension in his shoulders easing as he pulled her into a gentle embrace. Charlotte felt safe, cradled in his strong arms, the world around them fading into the background.

They stood there, lost in the warmth of their newfound confession, the weight of their shared experiences binding them together in a way neither could have anticipated. In that moment, the doubts and uncertainties that had once consumed Charlotte seemed to fade, replaced by a renewed sense of purpose and the unwavering support of the man she had come to love.

Charlotte felt a surge of emotion, the weight of their shared journey and the promise of a future intertwined etching itself upon her heart. Reaching up, she gently pulled Alexander close, sealing their declaration with a tender kiss.

In that moment, the world around them seemed to slow, the worries and expectations that had been pressing in on Charlotte melting away as she lost herself in the warmth of Alexander's embrace. For now, there was only the two of them, their bond forged through the crucible of adversity and strengthened by the depth of their feelings.

When they finally parted, their eyes shone with a newfound clarity, the path ahead no longer obscured by uncertainty, but illuminated by the promise of the future they would build, side by side.

Charlotte, the orphan, was home indeed.

The End

Printed in Great Britain
by Amazon